the Beach Cottage

CORAL ISLAND
BOOK TWO

LILLY MIRREN

BLACK LAB PRESS

Epub ISBN: 978-1-922650-14-6

Paperback ISBN: 978-1-922650-16-0

Version 1.0

Published by Black Lab Press 2022

Lilly Mirren has asserted her right to be identified as the author of this Work in accordance with the Copyright, Designs and Patents Act 1988.

This is a work of fiction. Names, characters, organisations, places, events and incidents are either products of the author's imagination or are used fictitiously. Any resemblance to actual persons, living or dead, or actual events is purely coincidental.

Cover design by Erin D'Ameron Hill.

First published worldwide by Black Lab Press in 2022.

Brisbane, Australia.

www.blacklabpress.com

One

THE GIRL LOOKED JUST like Aidan Whitlock.
Especially those long, spindly legs. That's what ran through
Beatrice Rushton's mind when the teenager confronted them
on the beach beside the roaring flames of a bonfire at her
housewarming party. The cottage was lit up by the glow of a
few lights she'd flicked on before she stepped outside to greet
her guests. She'd also lined the pathway down to the beach
with solar lanterns.

Guests meandered along the path, drinks in hand as they
chatted and laughed. Several milled around the food table
where she'd laid out a spread of finger foods, including olives,
cheeses, crackers, breads and dips.

None of that mattered in the moment. The party faded
into the background of Bea's thoughts as she turned her focus
back to her boyfriend and the girl standing before him.

What had she said?

You're my dad.

Bea glanced around at her group of friends — Evie, Taya
and Penny all gaped, eyes wide.

Aidan took the teen to one side and spoke to her in

1

hushed tones, one hand on her shoulder, his head bent low towards hers. Bea no longer had the comfort of his arm around her shoulders. She was the outsider, looking in on a private conversation between two people she didn't know. She thought she knew Aidan, but in that moment, he seemed a stranger to her. She shivered in the cool night air and hugged herself as Evie came up alongside her.

"Are you okay?"

Bea nodded. "Of course, I'm fine. I'm sure it's a misunderstanding. She must be about fifteen or so. Aidan was married fifteen years ago, and I know he wouldn't have cheated on his wife. We've had so many conversations about my marriage breakdown, and he's always expressed disgust at Preston's affair."

Evie patted her arm. "I'm sure you're right. He'll get to the bottom of this. Perhaps she made a mistake. What was her name again?"

"She introduced herself as Grace Allen and said her mother's name is Kelly Allen. Aidan's never mentioned a Kelly to me. Has he said anything to you about her?"

Evie shook her head. "I didn't really see much of him fifteen years ago. He lived in Brisbane then."

The girl reached for her long, golden hair and twirled it between her hands while Aidan said something to her in a muffled tone. Bea wished she could take a few steps closer without being obvious. Perhaps then she'd be able to hear what they were saying to one another.

Her certainty wavered — maybe Aidan *had* been unfaithful to his wife. If so, that would change everything between the two of them. Bea's heart had been broken by her own husband's unfaithfulness. She wasn't sure she could stomach Aidan having done the same thing, especially when his wife had died of cancer several years later and wasn't there to confront him over it.

She shouldn't jump to conclusions. She'd give him a chance to defend himself. To tell her what'd happened. But she couldn't get over how much like him the teen girl looked — even the way she held herself, the way she looked up at him with a barely veiled rebelliousness flashing in her eyes. It was all so Aidan. Memories of him as a teen boy helping her sneak out of the house, or urging her to leap off a cliff into the ocean before following, or giving her a cigarette to try for the first time, flashed before her eyes. This girl was the spitting image of him. With a sigh, her shoulders slumped, and she turned on her heel to stride back in the direction of the cottage.

There was no point fighting it. Aidan had a daughter.

"Where are you going?" Evie asked, jogging to keep up with her.

"Let's get out of here. I can't bear to stay a moment longer."

"But it's your party," objected Taya with a frown as she hurried after them, with Penny close behind.

"I don't care," Bea replied. "I've got to go."

Grace Allen.

A name that Beatrice Rushton wouldn't soon forget. She paced back and forth in her bedroom, worrying a fingernail with her teeth. She stared at her phone where it rested on the dresser against the wall. Why hadn't Aidan called?

She'd left the party at her own beach cottage, with guests exchanging puzzled looks and the fire still burning, food on the tables and drinks cooling in buckets. She, Taya, Evie and Penny had all headed back to Evie's place, a small timber house only a few hundred metres away from her bookshop, to spend the night.

They'd debated what the revelation could mean until the

wee hours of the morning over glasses of wine and in between bites of cheesecake and chocolate. They'd raised so many questions, and Bea's anxiety levels rose exponentially with each hour that passed until finally, she'd declared herself exhausted and headed to bed on the couch in the den.

Before she left the party, she'd locked the cottage door and left Aidan with the key. He promised to clean up the beach and send the rest of the guests home. She'd had to feed and water the pademelon that Penny had brought back from the wildlife refuge, then took it up to her father's house so he could care for the creature for a few days. She didn't have the capacity to care for it and was hardly home lately. He seemed quietly excited at the prospect and was already putting together a meal of leaves and vegetables when she left.

"Good luck," she'd whispered as she pulled the door shut behind her with a sigh of relief.

She'd forgotten to pack pyjamas or a toothbrush. Hadn't thought of anything much other than getting out of there. The idea of facing anyone after what'd happened was more than she could take.

They'd all seen it. Been witness to her humiliation.

She pressed both hands to her face and rubbed her eyes. This was insane. Why didn't he call? Surely he knew they had to talk. If nothing else, she wanted the truth. It might mean their relationship, as young and tender as it was, wouldn't last. But she deserved to know. He had to understand that, given the fact that her own husband had lied to, cheated on and stolen from her, she wouldn't stand for secrets in a relationship.

Maybe she shouldn't have left. Instead, she could've stayed and listened to the girl's explanation. It might have been a joke, but she didn't wait around to find out. Perhaps it was nothing, or maybe she'd misheard. *No*, she'd definitely heard her say the words, "I'm your daughter." And the similarities between her and Aidan were difficult to ignore.

This was Aidan Whitlock she was talking about. Aidan, who'd never had children. At least, that's what he'd told her and everyone else. His wife had died of cancer five years earlier. They'd been happy, he'd said. She vaguely recalled him mentioning that there had been ups and downs in their relationship, but any married couple could say the same thing.

She'd left Evie's place at first light and headed home. Aidan had left the key beneath her door mat and she found the party supplies neatly stowed in her kitchen, the dishes and glasses washed, and everything in its place. At least Aidan was a neat freak even if he did cheat on his wife. That was something, she supposed with a half-hearted smile.

If she didn't get out of the cottage, she'd go crazy thinking about it. Perhaps Aidan needed time to process what'd happened. She could give him that. It wasn't as though they'd been dating for very long. They were both adults—both had a past. No doubt he had some kind of explanation for what had occurred the previous evening. And there was no point in her wasting valuable energy pacing a path into her newly polished floorboards over it.

She showered quickly and dressed in a floral cotton frock with a matching belt. Breakfast was a bowl of homemade muesli and oat milk. She'd decided to go off dairy for a while to see if it would help with the constant congestion she'd had since she'd returned to the tropics. She'd forgotten how many allergies she could experience when living back in humidity and with thousands of blooming plants and trees around her every day of the week.

The news stories she flicked through on her iPad while eating did little to distract her. There was so much going on in the world, it was likely to give her indigestion if she took it all in. So instead, she turned off the iPad and made herself a coffee with her new coffee maker. Aidan had bought it for her as a housewarming gift for the cottage, and as the dark liquid poured into her enormous blue mug with *World's Greatest Mum* written on the side, she couldn't help thinking about how kind he'd been to do it.

Her ex-husband, Preston, had never bothered to buy her an espresso machine. In fact, he'd called the idea of ordering one wasteful because he didn't enjoy drinking coffee. But Aidan had purchased one without even asking her about it first and set it up in the cottage for her to enjoy. There were so many differences between him and Preston that she hardly knew where to start — but thoughtfulness was certainly one of the key distinctions.

After breakfast, she stepped outside and surveyed the cottage, her hands pressed to her hips. It was perfect. An idyllic beach cottage. She'd hired a contractor to renovate it when she moved to the island a year earlier after her husband left her for another woman. Coral Island was her childhood home. She'd spent so many years in the city that it took her a while to adjust to the idea of moving back here. But now that she'd established a life for herself on the island, she couldn't imagine living anywhere else, and wondered why it'd taken so long for her to return.

The cottage was painted white with blue accents. It was nestled among spindly bushes, sea grasses and pandanus trees behind the dunes that lined a private cove with white sand, azure waters shushing gently to shore and black rocky outcroppings marking either end. It'd been her home after she was born, up until her parents built a much larger house for their growing family on the headland above. Then it had fallen into disrepair after her mother died.

Dad didn't have the heart to rent it out to strangers since it'd been one of her mother's favourite haunts. But now it was Bea's home and she couldn't be happier with how the renovation had worked out — there was a modern kitchen and two bathrooms, as well as fresh paint and a large, sturdy verandah that looked out over the beach.

She spun around and strode forwards through the sand. She often took a walk along the beach in the mornings, as it gave her a chance to think about the day ahead and clear her thoughts. The morning had already heated up, and she was bathed in a light film of sweat when she came puffing back up the beach to the cottage half an hour later. Aidan's truck was there, parked beside the cottage. She hadn't locked up before she left, so she washed her feet at the tap on the side of the cottage then went right inside to find Aidan sitting at the kitchen table, sipping a cup of coffee.

He smiled up at her, half happy to see her, half hesitant. She understood the sentiment — she wasn't exactly sure how to broach this subject with him herself.

"Hi," she said.

He stood to greet her, kissing her forehead awkwardly.

She pushed away from him and filled a glass with water from the tap, downing it in two long gulps.

"I thought you might be walking."

"You know me well."

He nodded. "I thought we should talk about last night."

"Good idea." She sat opposite him at the table.

"It seems I have a daughter."

Beatrice arched an eyebrow but didn't speak.

He offered her a wan smile. "I'm sure you gathered that much."

"I thought maybe she was a fan at first..."

"Not a fan. It turns out that an old relationship resulted in a pregnancy I knew nothing about."

"But weren't you married?" She asked the question as gently as she could. She didn't want to make any kind of judgement about his relationship. They'd barely spoken about

7

his marriage until this point. After all, his wife had died, and he'd grieved her a long time. It wasn't exactly a topic Bea felt comfortable raising in casual conversation.

He rubbed his chin. "Yes, I was married. But we were separated. It was long before she got sick, and we tried to work things out. But she told me it was over, that she couldn't keep going the way it was, with me so focused on my career. She felt lost, she was lonely, she wanted to go home to live with her parents. We fought a lot. It was a difficult time for me, but she moved out and I thought my marriage was over. I really believed that."

Bea inhaled a slow breath. "I knew you'd never have cheated on your wife that way."

"Thank you," he replied, relief written across his face. "I don't want there to be any confusion because of how your husband treated you. But the fact is, I did cheat. We weren't divorced, but I thought we were on our way towards divorce. The affair showed me how much I loved my wife — I missed her, I wanted to work things out. So, I broke off the affair with Kelly and went to see my wife, begging her to try again. And we did. The rest is history."

"And Kelly?"

"I never heard from her after that. She told me she was moving back to Adelaide to be with her family, and that was the last time we spoke."

Bea stood and paced to the other side of the kitchen, then back again. "This is crazy. You have a teenaged daughter, and you knew nothing about her?"

"Nothing." He raised his hands in mock surrender. "I swear. But honestly, I'm kind of excited. I know the timing isn't great, but I thought I'd never have children. I'd come to terms with it. Heck, for a long time I even told myself it was for the best, that I could give my career my full attention. But I've always wanted a child."

"She's almost grown."

"I know." He shook his head. "I'm trying not to be angry at Kelly for keeping her from me. I missed out on so much."

"I'm sorry," Bea simply said. She reached out a hand to Aidan, and he took it, squeezed it.

"Thank you. I really want to spend some time getting to know her. I've missed her entire childhood. I can't think about anything else right now."

Bea nodded. "Of course. I understand." She could see it in his eyes. He was breaking up with her before they'd even had a chance to try. But she couldn't argue—she didn't want to get in between him and his daughter.

"I knew you would. We can revisit things when I've had some time to process it all and get to know Grace a little better."

"We'll talk then."

Bea swallowed around the lump in her throat as she watched Aidan walk away. He climbed into his truck and waved goodbye, then backed out of her driveway. She stood staring after him, her eyes full of tears.

Their reconciliation had been too good to be true. All this time, she'd wanted to take things slowly between them so she was ready and wouldn't hurt him. But she hadn't realised it would be him who'd hurt her, and so soon.

With a shake of her head, she walked back to her bedroom to take a shower. She had a busy day planned, and there was no point standing around moping. There was work to be done.

Two

THE SHOVEL SEEMED HEAVIER in Penny St James' hands with every passing moment. She pushed it as deep into the soft ground as she could manage, then jumped up and down on the edge of it until it was embedded in the squelching mud. She levered it back and forth, finding it was wedged a little too far into the mud now. It took all her weight and several minutes before she was able to budge the shovel, and finally it came flying out of the ground, sending her stumbling backwards.

She landed on her rear end in the mud with a thwack. The shovel fell at her feet. Mud oozed up through her pants. She grimaced and pushed her hands against the earth to gain her feet only to find that her hands were stuck in the mud entirely. So much for her manicure. She knew better than to get one since she ran a wildlife refuge, but her parents had given her a gift certificate for the spa at the new resort over in Blue Shoal for Christmas, and she'd put it to use the previous day with a facial, massage and manicure. It'd been heavenly. But now her blue glitter nail polish was buried wrist-deep in sucking black mud.

Nearby, a large grey kangaroo stood staring at her.

"Come on, Frank, give me a hand, will you? Or a paw?" She wrinkled her nose. It itched on the end, but she couldn't reach to scratch it. Her hands were still stuck in the mud, and even if they weren't, she'd end up with black muck across her face. Instead, she wriggled her nose back and forth, the itch quickly becoming unbearable.

A strand of honey-blonde hair fell across her face, covering one brown eye. She blew it, sending it back for a moment, but it fell into place again just as fast.

"Ugh. Now what?" she murmured to herself. Alison, her assistant, was inside, feeding the snakes. She wouldn't hear if Penny called, and besides, there was one rule about snake feeding at the refuge — don't let yourself be interrupted by anyone or anything. Penny had implemented the rule when one of the volunteers had stopped what they were doing to answer the gate and they'd lost a python in the break room for a full hour. It'd been a stressful day, and one Penny hoped never to repeat. Especially since the python had almost made it out to the kangaroo enclosure, where there were wallabies and other small creatures just waiting to be eaten.

She wriggled one hand free, then the other. She couldn't help giggling. With the kangaroo watching her intently, she laughed heartily at herself. She was completely stuck. There was no way to get out of there without help unless she somehow made it onto her knees. Just as she was about to try, she heard the front gate click shut.

"Hello! Who's there?"

"Penny?" A man's voice sounded through the enclosure, one she didn't immediately recognise. "Where are you?"

"This way," she called.

A handsome face appeared, thick brown hair and large brown eyes above a stubbled chin. Rowan Clements, the man who'd humiliated her as a teenager and whose presence always invoked anger deep down in her gut. A smirk flickered across his handsome features. "What are you doing?"

"Taking a bath. What does it look like?"

Rowan stopped short, crossed his arms. "I can leave you here if you're going to be like that."

"No, please — I need help," she admitted. There was no time for pleasantries or for the obvious question — what was he doing in her wildlife sanctuary? The front gate was locked, and only people with the code could gain entrance unless someone was manning the reception desk. Which no one was at that moment, since there were only two of them on-site — she was stuck in the mud, and Alison was ankle-deep in snakes.

He laughed quietly as he surveyed her. "Now, how did you manage that?"

She held out her hands. "I'll tell you all about it just as soon as you get me out of here."

He wore a pair of expensive blue jeans and a buttoned shirt. His hair was casually mussed and his physique was perfectly athletic and tanned. She'd seen him recently on television — intrepid reporter and high school nemesis. He was a man of many faces. And she itched to punch him in every single one of them.

"Rowan Clements, get over here and help me."

He winked. "You know, I've been gone for years and yet here you are, still in the same place I left you, doing the same thing. You always seem to find yourself in trouble right as I come along. My very own damsel in distress."

She rolled her eyes. The last time she'd seen Rowan in person, he'd rescued her from a rip in the ocean. Hardly the same situation, but it irked her to be in need of rescuing again in that moment. She wasn't the kind of woman to get herself into scrapes that required help, and the fact that he thought of her as one, only further irritated her.

"That was an entirely different situation. I got caught in a rip—a few of us did. And anyway, you were barely any help at all."

"Maybe, or perhaps you'd have drowned if I didn't rescue you. I guess we'll never know. I'm sure in a few years, you'll pretend you didn't need me to get you out of this mud as well." He reached forward and clasped both of her hands, then began to pull while he straddled the mud as best as he could to avoid getting his expensive shoes dirty.

Penny was willing to put all their differences aside for the moment just to get out of the muck. It'd leached into her pants, coated both legs and was climbing up her back at that very moment. As Rowan pulled, there was a great sucking sound, and she began to shift in his direction.

"Yes, that's it — keep going!"

"What is that kangaroo up to?" Rowan asked, eyeing Frank.

The creature sidled around behind Rowan, fists raised as it bounced lightly on large hind legs.

"Frank, don't you dare!" Penny recognised the stance. It was Frank's boxing pose. He didn't like men in his enclosure, and normally Penny would've warned anyone who came in to keep their distance, but in this case, they'd had no choice.

"Don't dare what? What's he doing?" Rowan tried to look over his shoulder but couldn't see the animal.

"Frank!" Penny used her most stern voice, but it was no use. Frank wasn't listening. He rocked onto his tail and kicked with both hind feet into the middle of Rowan's back.

Rowan's eyes widened and he fell directly onto Penny, knocking her down as he went. She landed with her ponytail in the mud. With a grunt, he caught himself with both hands pressed on either side of her. His face hovered above hers, his breath warm on her skin.

"Frank, stop it!" Penny screeched.

The kangaroo wandered off. Penny glared at Rowan.

"What? It's not my fault," he said, grinning down at her. "Although I'm not complaining."

His mouth was dangerously close to Penny's, and she stared at his full lips a moment before pressing both hands to his chest and pushing hard. He was far too heavy for her to lift, and the effort merely left handprints on his formerly clean shirt. She wriggled to no avail. He appeared to be laughing at her, although he didn't make a sound. Why was everything about him so obnoxiously irritating? And why was he still on top of her?

"Can you *please* move?"

He struggled to his feet with a flash of white teeth, then pulled her free of the mud. "I can't believe I'm covered in this junk within the first twenty seconds of visiting you. You really are something, Penny St James. Life's never dull when you're around."

Mud dripped from both of them. Penny couldn't help feeling a little satisfaction in seeing his perfectly styled outfit covered in muck. She suppressed a smile. "I aim to please."

"You're loving this, aren't you?"

"Of course not," she huffed. "And besides, what did you expect would happen, coming to a wildlife refuge dressed like you've stepped out of *GQ Magazine*?" She squeezed the mud from her ponytail.

"You think I look like a model?" He quirked an eyebrow.

She rolled her eyes. Trust Rowan to take it as a compliment. He had always been full of himself. There were times when Penny had wondered why she'd disliked him so much in high school, but as soon as she spent time with him, it all came rushing back. He was infuriating, frustrating, irritating and about a thousand other things she didn't have time to think of right in that moment.

She had to get cleaned up and finish building the enclosure she'd been in the middle of making for the new kangaroo that'd been brought in that morning with her joey. Penny wanted to dig a small billabong for them so they'd be able to drink in a more natural environment, but the amount of rain they'd had lately had left the area she'd earmarked for it a muddy swampland.

"What are you doing here, anyway?" she asked as she strode to the closest building, Rowan beside her.

"I came with Rob."

"Rob's here?" Her brother had been living on the mainland for months and had promised to come home, but she hadn't seen him yet. She missed him so much when he was gone on a work trip, but she hated to admit it to Rowan. At least that answered the question of how Rowan made it through the locked front gate.

"Yeah, he and I came in on the ferry this morning."

"Together?"

"Just a coincidence. He finished up the construction project he was working on, and I'm taking some time off between jobs, so I thought I'd come home for a while."

"I bet your mum is happy to see you."

He shrugged. "I guess. She's never really happy these days, but I wanted to see her anyway."

Rob stood waiting by the door, tapping at something on his phone screen. He looked up in surprise at the two of them as they approached.

"What on earth?"

"We had an incident," Rowan replied.

"I can see that. Quite the welcome there, sis." Rob shook his head. "I'd give you a hug, but..."

Her brother was tall and muscular. He wore a perpetually mischievous smile, and his personality matched the smile to perfection.

"Why'd you bring him?" she asked, dipping her head in Rowan's direction while she fished in her pocket for keys.

"Nice manners," Rowan replied.

"Come on—it's time to bury the hatchet. Don't you think?" Rob said.

She unlocked the door. "He humiliated me in front of the entire school. It's not something you forget."

"It was twenty-five years ago," Rowan objected. "You can't still hold that against me."

He had a point. Perhaps it was time for her to let it go and move on. After all, they'd both been teenagers at the time, and she was ready to admit she'd done more than a few silly and thoughtless things as a teen. She'd decided to weed the drama out of her life lately, to become more mature and to grow as a person. She read somewhere that's what people did in their forties, and since she'd passed the halfway mark in that decade, she figured it was time she took the plunge herself. "Fine, I suppose I can put it behind me. It was a long time ago."

"Finally. Thank you." Rowan grinned. "Of course, now I'll have this roll in the mud to hold over your head for the rest of time. Anyhoo, I'm going to head home and grab a shower and a change of clothes. Lovely to see you as always, Pen."

He gave a mock bow and walked away. Penny watched him go, agape. She never could think of a retort when Rowan was around. It was as though all the clever words floated right out of her head and there was only a big, wide blank space between her ears.

"He still gets under your skin, I see," Rob said.

She shook her head. "Not at all. I'm perfectly at ease."

He laughed and leaned over to kiss the only clean spot on her forehead. "It's good to see you again, sis. I've missed you."

Three

THERE WAS one thing in Beatrice's life that was working out the way she'd intended. Her marriage might have fallen apart, her children had left home, her boyfriend had broken up with her, but her brand-new business venture was taking shape, and a buzz of excitement sent her heart into a flutter any time she thought about it.

The renovations on the café were going to plan. She loved the look of the place. It was attached to the side of Eveleigh's Books, a small boutique bookshop run by one of her best high school friends. And with the addition of the café, they were both hoping business would boom. There was a decided lack of decent coffee on the island, and Bea intended to fill that gap.

The bookshop was long and thin, with a set of stairs at the entrance. It was built in a style of timber that was reminiscent of old wooden docks, just as the attached café was. It'd been painted in blues and whites, with natural timber shining through in places as well. And there was an old ship's wheel attached to the front of the shop. Bea wondered if it confused customers who were looking for books, but the bookshop seemed to do a roaring trade, so people must've found it without too much difficulty.

Her contractor was almost finished, and Bea was helping out by oiling the hardwood bench in the newly renovated kitchen. She pushed her hair back behind her shoulders and sighed. A bead of sweat trickled down the side of her face beneath the scarf wrapped around her hair. The February heat was getting to Bea. She'd managed to survive an entire summer on the island with plenty of dips in the ocean and lots of evening walks along the beach in the ocean breeze, but the humidity the past week had been unbearable.

"It's looking good in here." Eveleigh poked her head around a drop cloth separating the bookshop from the café. Her shiny red hair swung ahead of her shoulders, her fringe dangling across her large brown eyes. Usually she wore it in tight curls, today it was straight.

"Thanks. I think so too. I'm really excited about how everything's coming together."

"I'm making coffee. Would you like one?" Evie's invitation came at the perfect time. Bea's back ached, her knees were sore from squatting and bending so much, and her head was light since she'd forgotten to eat lunch.

She wiped her hands on the apron around her waist and set down her paintbrush. "That would be great."

Bea followed Evie into the small kitchen behind the bookshop and sat at the round table while Evie got to work making coffees for both of them. There was a clean cloth draped over a cake in the centre of the table, and Evie pulled it back. "Hummingbird cake?"

"Wow. You made this? It looks delicious."

"Thanks. I hope it is. It's my grandmother's recipe. One of the few things I make well."

Bea sliced two pieces and set them on mismatched china plates.

Evie handed her a mug of steaming coffee with chocolate-sprinkled froth on top and sat opposite her with a sigh. "My feet hurt."

"How's the bookshop today?" Bea took a bite of cake. The moist flavour burst across her tongue — pineapple, cinnamon and coconut.

"Busy, which is good. But I'm trying to do some research at the same time, and it's hard to concentrate with all those customers interrupting me constantly."

Bea laughed. "What are you researching?"

"Those photos you had me develop. The fifty-year-old ones you and Dani found in the kitchen wall when you were renovating your cottage. I kept a copy of them for myself—I hope you don't mind. And I've been trying to identify everyone in the images." Evie's dimples deepened as she spoke.

"Wow. I didn't realise you were doing that. I think it's a great idea. Have you had any luck?"

"Actually, I have. You know how we figured that it was Penny's beach house in the photos?"

Bea nodded, chewing.

"Well, I decided to go back through every record I could find with photographs of her beach house and her family to see if I could identify the people in them. We already identified Rowan's mum, June, so that made the job a little easier."

"I love this. It's like you're a spy or something." Bea took a sip of coffee.

Evie reached for an envelope, pulled the photographs out and laid them on the table. "So, in this one, we've got a whole lot of people — these are the ones I've identified so far. This is June Clements. This stern-looking woman is her mother. I'm not sure who these people are, but this man seems to be Rowan's dad."

"Oh, and that other lady is Penny's mother, I think. At least, that's what Penny said, although she's much younger than the last time I saw her. And the woman behind her is Penny's grandmother, but I never knew her. She died when we were all very young."

"She was murdered, right?"

Bea's nose wrinkled. "Yep, but I can't recall any of the details. We were so young, and Penny never talks about her."

"I'm going to the library later to see if I can find some resources — maybe an old newspaper article or something."

"I'll come with you." Bea finished her cup of coffee. "I could use a distraction."

"How're things going with Aidan?"

She shrugged. "He wants us to take some time apart."

"Already?"

"Yep. Says he needs to spend the time getting to know his daughter and he can't give our relationship the attention it deserves."

Evie grimaced. "Oh, I'm sorry, honey."

"It's fine—we were moving too quickly anyway. I wasn't ready for the kind of relationship he wanted."

"So, maybe it's for the best?" Evie squeezed her shoulder.

"Maybe, but it still hurts."

"There's a chance you'll be able to work things out, though."

Bea sighed. "I hope so. The more time we spend apart, the more I realise how much I care about him. It's funny—before he broke things off, I was so cautious about moving forward and wanted to make sure I was ready so I wouldn't hurt him. But every day that we're apart, it's like there's this wound that's opened up inside me and it aches more and more."

Evie shook her head. "It's all going to work out. Trust me, the two of you are meant to be together. Everyone can see that."

"Do you think so?"

"Absolutely. Who is more perfectly suited than the two of

you? If it hadn't been for—well, what happened when you were a teenager, the two of you would've never broken up."

"You mean Mum's death."

"Sorry, I didn't mean to bring that up. I'm just pouring salt into those wounds, aren't I?" Evie wrung her hands together.

Bea laughed. "It's okay. It was a long time ago. I can talk about Mum's death now without wanting to crawl into a hole and cry for hours. These days I ask myself what she might think or do whenever I'm not sure about something. I don't want to forget her. She was an extraordinary person."

"You're right about that," Evie said, her eyes gleaming. "It was a hard time for everyone. None of us knew how to help you, least of all Aidan. I think if that hadn't happened, the two of you would've gotten married and spent your lives together. You loved each other so much. This is just another bump in the road, but you'll find your way back to each other."

"I hope you're right. But for now, I'm focused on getting this café up and running. What do you think about sticky date puddings for the menu?"

"That sounds perfect. Oh, by the way, we always mark the end of summer at Point Prospect with a dip off the headland with the dolphins. Are you up for it? We're going next week."

Bea frowned. "You still do that?"

"Every February." Evie laughed. "Surely you're not too old."

Bea felt too old to do a lot of things these days. But for so many years, she'd opted out of taking risks, or having fun, or doing the things she wanted to do because she was more concerned with what her husband wanted or her children needed. It was time to do some things for herself, and if that meant frolicking in the waves with dolphins or jumping off the headland into the surf, she wasn't going to miss out. She'd always been an adventurer, but she'd pushed that part of herself aside for so long, she'd forgotten how. "Okay. Count me in."

* * *

Once Bea had finished up for the day, she stepped outside to feel the sea breeze on her face. The humidity level had dropped, and it was a lovely evening, with the sun setting over the distant mainland in a blaze of orange and pink.

A ferry pulled away from the dock, leaving a trail of white foaming waves in its wake. A car was parked beside the primary school, and a teen girl climbed out. Spindly legs stuck out from a pair of white denim shorts. Her long brown hair bounced down her back in a ponytail. She walked to the gate and waited.

Bea's heart leapt into her throat. It was Grace. Aidan's daughter looked just like him from that distance. She was the image of his teen silhouette with the setting sun behind her. Tall, lanky, athletic, but with long hair and a crop top.

Just then, Aidan walked out of the school with a briefcase beneath his arm. His sleeves were rolled up, exposing muscular forearms. His hair was messy, and he grinned at Grace. He embraced her, and they walked together back to the car, deep in conversation. He glanced up and noticed Bea watching them. Her cheeks blazed with the embarrassment of being caught out. He raised a hand in greeting, and she waved back. Then he climbed into the car with Grace, and they drove away.

Bea's heart thudded against her rib cage. This was going to be more difficult than she'd realised. She hated that they lived on the same small island together and she couldn't be with him. Couldn't call to talk about her day or ask him what he thought about the photographs she and Evie had discussed. Hated that they were being pulled apart by something that'd happened fifteen years ago, back before she'd even realised they might get a second chance at a life together.

For so long, she'd buried her feelings for him because he'd walked away from her and she'd had her heart broken. But now that he'd told her how he felt, he'd opened that door again, and her heart had reawakened. She wasn't sure she could go through the pain of heartbreak all over again. Especially not so soon after losing her twenty-five-year-long marriage.

But she had no choice. She had to keep putting one foot in front of the other. There was no alternative. Besides, she'd promised Dad she would cook dinner for him and Bradford that night. Even though she was exhausted, she was looking forward to seeing them both. One of the benefits of moving back to Coral Island was that she had renewed her relationships with both her father and her brother — relationships she'd let wane for far too long due to misunderstandings and her own fear of returning to the place where she'd suffered so much loss in childhood.

Her phone rang, and she pressed it to her ear as she returned to the café to look for her purse.

"Hi, Mum." Danita's voice brought a wave of affection. She missed her daughter already.

"Danita Pike, fancy hearing from you so soon." Her daughter had flown back Sydney only a few days earlier to begin her new university degree. "How is interior design going? Have you made the world beautiful already?"

Danita grunted. "Very funny, Mum. I was wondering if you'd had a chance to put that money into my account for the textbooks we talked about."

"I should've known this phone call would be about money, and yes, it's in your account." Bea slung her handbag over her shoulder.

"Sorry, Mum. How are you? How's the café?"

"I'm fine. I miss Aidan already, but I'll survive. And the café is almost finished. I can't believe how quickly it's all coming together. I should be able to open within a month or so, I think. If I can find some staff."

"Well, I'll help out during the holidays."

"I'm glad to hear it." Bea smiled. Sometimes everything felt overwhelming. And at other times, she was grateful and truly believed it would work out. At the moment, she was sitting somewhere in between both poles.

They chatted for a few minutes, and then she hung up the phone as she walked to the old station wagon she'd borrowed from her father. He said she could have it, since he had no need of it. He had his truck to get around, so she'd put off buying herself a vehicle. There wasn't much need for one on the island unless she intended to go across to Blue Shoal. And for that, she'd either need the entire day to circumnavigate the island or a four-wheel drive to cross it. She'd begun to think that buying a boat would be a better and far more enjoyable use of her resources.

So far, she'd had to rely on other people to drive her across the island. But since her move, she'd decided she should become more independent — she'd given far too much of her trust to Preston over the years, had relied on him and had regretted it. She was an independent woman now and in the spirit of independence she'd have to learn to do more herself. And that included buying a boat so she could navigate the island on her own.

Four

BEA SQUEEZED the pastry between her fingers and set the dumpling aside. Then she reached for another circular casing. She pushed the pork and chives mixture into a clump at the centre of the dumpling, closed the pastry around it and pressed it shut with her fingers. There was something so therapeutic about making dumplings — the repetitive nature of it, the mundanity. It'd always been one of her family's favourite dishes. The kids still asked for it when they came home for holidays.

Her father's kitchen was a little dated, but it was spacious and well-equipped and one of her favourite places to work, since it had large picture windows that looked out across the ocean and she could stand at the bench and enjoy the view while she cooked. She also loved his marble bench tops in charcoal with grey streaks — they were a complete contrast to the latest trend of building everything in sterile white, as were the dark timber cabinets.

"What are you making there, honey?" Dad came up behind her, his hair dripping wet from the shower. He peered over her shoulder.

"Gyoza."

"Huh?"

"Dumplings," she replied with a smile, setting another dumpling on the plate.

"Oh, right. Looks nice."

"You like dumplings, don't you?"

"Not sure. Don't think I've ever had them."

She frowned. "Really? Well, I think you'll like them. They're very tasty."

"I'll take your word for it." He walked into the lounge room and sat in his armchair with a sigh. "That feels better." He raised the footrest and leaned back, eyes shut.

"Busy day?" Bea asked.

He nodded. "I did some slashing in the bottom paddock. The grass got really high this summer with all the rain."

"Didn't the neighbours used to bring their horses over to help keep the grass down for you?"

"They've been a bit slack this year. I think they sold a couple of them and haven't replaced them yet. The girls are in pony club, but not sure how much longer they'll be doing it. They've almost finished high school."

"Wow. Time flies," Bea said.

"How's the cottage?" Dad asked.

"It's great," Bea replied. "I love it there. It's so tranquil. I feel like I'm on an extended holiday. I miss having Dani around, but it's good to know she's back in Sydney studying to do something she loves. I don't want her to miss out on anything."

"The way you did?" Dad opened one eye to peer at her.

Bea's lips pulled into a straight line. "I suppose so. I don't regret having the children, of course. But maybe I should've waited a little longer — done some things for myself."

"There's no time like the present."

Bea laughed. "What — you think I should go to university now? I'm not too old?"

He huffed. "Of course you're not too old. If you want to study something, change course, go for it. But if you like what you're doing, then don't. I think it's important not to have regrets. Especially when you can do something about it. If there's something you've always wished you could do, now's the best time to do it. The kids are grown, you've got a little nest egg saved up, you don't have a husband to think of..."

Her heart squeezed at his words. She didn't have anyone to think of any longer. Only herself. Now that her husband had moved on with his mistress and her boyfriend had broken up with her to spend time getting to know his new daughter, she was completely alone in the world.

Dad studied her face. "Sorry, honey. I didn't mean to strike a nerve. But you get my point."

She set the plate of dumplings aside. "You're right, of course. Not having anyone in my life gives me the opportunity to make choices I might not have made otherwise. I should try to look at it as a positive thing."

"That's my girl."

"But I think the cafe is a good start for me. It's something I've always wanted to do."

"I'm proud of you," he said.

Bea continued working, and in a few minutes, she heard the faint sounds of snoring coming from Dad's armchair. She smiled and went to pull a knitted blanket over his legs before returning to the kitchen to continue slicing vegetables.

A truck pulled into the driveway. Bea heard the engine growl before it switched off. A few moments later, her younger brother, Bradford, barrelled through the front door.

"Hello? Anyone home?"

"In the kitchen," she said.

He found her there and wrapped her in a bear hug, lifting her feet from the ground. "How's my little sister?"

Ever since he was fifteen years old, he'd towered over her and liked to joke about her being the little sister.

She laughed, slapping his shoulder playfully. "Put me down, you giant." They'd struggled to get along over the years, but after some long overdue discussions where they confessed their concerns and insecurities, they were doing their best to put the past behind them.

They'd both agreed to build a new, more mature relationship that didn't involve bringing up the pain of the past as a battering ram to use against one another whenever they were irritated or frustrated.

He spied the plate of dumplings. "Yum! That looks delicious. I heard you were cooking, and I knew I couldn't miss it. These days, I don't get much in the way of home-cooked meals made by someone other than myself. And I tend to be lazy and throw salad and fish on a plate most nights."

"Not exactly lazy when you've been working all day," Bea said.

He shrugged. "True. But then I eat half a loaf of bread because the salad isn't enough and I'm starving."

"Sounds about right," Bea replied with a grin. "So, I'm going to fatten you up tonight. I've got gyoza, san choi bow, stir-fried barramundi and coconut rice."

He licked his lips. "I can't wait. How's the café coming?"

"It's good. The renovations are almost done. Actually, I thought I should probably have a grand opening or something. Would you like to come?"

"Of course. That's a great idea. I can help—just let me know what you need from the mainland and I'll get it for you. I'm there every day for work."

"Sounds like business is booming."

He nodded. "We can barely keep up. Every single one of

the boats is booked. We've got people sailing around the islands, or deep-sea fishing, or even holding corporate events on the water. I'll probably have to expand, but I don't want to overextend myself, so we're trying to keep up as best we can right now."

"Sounds wise," she said. "Do you remember when we were kids and we used to swim with the dolphins off Point Prospect every summer to mark the end of the school holidays?"

He grabbed a beer from the fridge and popped the lid. "Yes, of course. It was fun."

"Apparently, some of them are still doing it. Evie invited me to go with them next week. You should come too."

He took a gulp of beer. "I'd like that. I'll bring one of the yachts, and we can make a day of it."

"That would be amazing," Bea said. "I'll let Evie know. We can pack a picnic."

"It'll be much more civilised than it used to be, when we'd starve for half the day and then someone would scrounge up a few dollars to buy hot chips at the local corner shop."

"Much more civilised." She washed a strainer full of rice in the sink before putting it in the rice cooker and switching it on.

"Hey, has Dad talked to you about his health lately?" Bradford leaned against the bench, crossing one foot over the other.

Bea's brow furrowed. "What do you mean?"

"He really should talk to you about it. It's not my place to say anything."

Bea stopped what she was doing and spun to face Bradford. "Brad, spill it. What's going on?"

He sighed. "Dad's been having some dizzy spells and not feeling great in general. They're running tests, but they're not sure what's wrong with him yet. I told him to talk to you about it, but he thinks it'll only worry you."

"Of course it worries me!" Bea shouted.

"Shhhh!" Bradford waved a hand. "He's sleeping."

"Of course it worries me," Bea repeated in a whisper. "I can't believe he'd keep that from me. I had no idea he wasn't feeling well."

"Don't make a big deal of it. Okay?"

"Fine, but I have to say something so he knows that I know. Otherwise, he'll just keep pretending everything's okay."

As Bradford walked out onto the deck, Bea watched him go with her heart racing. What if there was something really wrong with Dad? She'd missed spending time with him in recent years. Missed so much. And now that they'd finally reconciled and were able to see each other as often as they liked, what if he was sick and that time would be cut short? She couldn't lose him yet. It was far too soon.

She shook her head and turned her attention back to dinner preparation. She was being overly dramatic. There might be a completely innocent explanation for what was going on with him. She didn't know what was wrong or what it would mean for any of them. But even so, her anxiety levels spiked as she worked.

She would talk to him about it, but not tonight. Tonight, they could enjoy a nice meal together as a family, just the three of them. She only wished she'd done that more often instead of being so focused on her life in the city for the past two decades. But there was no going back; she could only move forward and do things differently from now on. Beating herself up over the past wouldn't achieve anything. She glanced at her father's sleeping form in the armchair, and a wave of emotion washed over her.

Five

THE DRIVE to the Blue Shoal Inn was best avoided. Instead, Penny climbed into the boat that was moored at the dock outside her beach house and drove it around the island. As she pulled away from the dock, she looked back at her house where it squatted amongst a thicket of she-oaks and semi-tropical rainforest. A large verandah along the back of the beach house was hung with climbing roses. She adored the beach house, it was her happy place.

Her parents had given it to her when they'd moved into a small unit in Cairns, and she'd spent the past few years doing it up a little bit at a time. She loved the peacefulness of the place, the way the beach behind the house was a private oasis that tourists rarely stumbled across. She loved that it was hers and that the rambling internal structure had been like a cubby with plenty of hiding spots when she was a kid. She'd loved exploring every room, nook and crevice with a stuffed toy under one arm admits the echoes of her mother playing the piano.

The boat pushed through the small waves that chortled to shore. The surf was always light, since the island was sheltered by the Great Barrier Reef. The boat surged over a low wave and then settled into the choppy ocean beyond. A southeasterly wind had picked up early that morning and still buffeted the shoreline.

Penny raised a hand to hold her hat in place as she drove one-handed around the island. It really was a beautiful sight, Coral Island with the midday sun glistening on azure waters and steep cliffs of red and brown clay intermingled with black rocks rising from the depths to her left.

She slowed her pace to pull the boat into the marina at Blue Shoal, letting her hand drop back to her side, her hat safe. The boat idled through the marina, and she stopped in an empty space then tethered the boat in place.

"Penny St James? Seeing you twice in the space of a week can't be a coincidence." Rowan's deep voice startled her and had her heart racing before she'd even turned to face him.

Her cheeks flushed with warmth at the sight of him standing beside a boat on the timber dock, shirtless and wearing a cap, his sweaty torso glistening beneath the sun's warm rays. He held a rope in one hand. His abdominal muscles were tight and toned.

"Hello again," she said awkwardly.

"What are you doing in my hometown?"

"You live in Blue Shoal?"

"Temporarily, of course."

"I thought you lived in New York or something."

"I did." He shrugged. "I'm taking some time to rethink my career direction."

"Is that code for being unemployed?" She shuddered at her own words. Why was she always so rude to him? He brought out the worst in her, and she couldn't understand why.

"I suppose you could say that." He laughed. "Unemployed and trying to figure out my next move."

"Don't you enjoy journalism anymore?"

He picked up a large rope and coiled it around his elbow and hand carefully. "Not as much as I did. There was a certain level of excitement to traveling and staying in hotels, chasing down leads and finding the story. But I'm older now, and I'd like to settle somewhere. Journalism doesn't really allow for that. Although since I'm not qualified to do anything else, I suppose I'll have to stick with it until I figure out what to do."

"I never thought I'd see the day that Rowan Clements would settle down." She shook her head. Next, he'd be saying he wanted to get married. And even though Penny had never taken the plunge herself, she'd always wanted to.

It'd been a source of immense frustration and disappointment over the years whenever long-term relationships had fizzled out or ended suddenly and without warning. Years that she'd dedicated to building connections, hoping it might end in a family of her own only to watch it all fall apart. She'd given up hoping and instead chose to be content with her animals and friendships these days.

He grinned. "I suppose stranger things have happened."

"That's true."

"So, you didn't answer my question. What are you doing in Blue Shoal?"

"I'm having lunch with some friends — Evie, Taya and Beatrice."

"The whole crew back together again," he said. "That must be nice."

"It's awesome, actually. I missed them for such a long time. Mostly it's only been me and Taya here, and for much of that, she was dealing with a lot in her own life, so I didn't see her often. But now we're all back on the island, and unbelievably, all single."

"Wow," he said, looking surprised. "It would be great to catch up with them. I haven't seen them in ages."

"You should come swimming with us at Point Prospect in a few days."

"Still marking the end of summer the same way?" He set the rope on the ground by his feet.

"That's right. We're going to swim with the dolphins."

"Text me the details. I'd love to join you."

"Perfect," she said, waving goodbye as she walked across the marina. "See you later."

She smiled to herself as she made her way through the quaint Main Street of Blue Shoal. That was the most mature and pleasant conversation she'd ever had with Rowan Clements. Maybe they were turning a corner. They were in their mid-forties, after all. If they couldn't work through their teen angst now, they never would. She felt good about it. They might not be close, but at least they could be cordial.

He was ridiculously attractive these days. She didn't recall him being quite so suave when they were young, but he'd grown into his looks very well. Of course, that was irrelevant—she wasn't interested in someone like him. No doubt he'd be on his way in a few days or weeks, back to the jet-setting lifestyle he'd always had. And she'd stay here on the island rescuing native animals. She had no desire to get involved with a man who never sat still. Sitting still was one of her favourite things to do.

And besides all that, her brother had a rule about friends dating his sister. He'd made a bit of a fuss about it when they were younger, but perhaps he'd put it behind him by now. Anyway, she doubted Rowan would be at all interested in her when it was likely he had a woman in every port.

The Blue Shoal Inn was one of Penny's favourite places on the entire island. It perched on a rise looking over a cozy cove at one end of the tiny village. It was in dire need of a paint job, but had a quaint and historic look that was popular with a certain segment of the tourist population who frequented this part of the island. Beyond the inn was a brand-new resort glistening white beneath the heat of the sun, apartments stepping up the hillside and turning the village into a modern complex with swimming pools, spas, palm trees and winding footpaths.

She found Taya, Evie and Beatrice seated in the private dining room at the back of the inn. They were already drinking their first cocktail. A grazing board sat in the centre of the table featuring various crackers, cheeses, breads and dips. Penny greeted them all with a hug and then reached for a piece of crusty bread, slathering it with camembert before collapsing into one of the chairs.

"It's good to sit down. I've had the craziest morning."

"Crazier than ending up in the mud with your high school crush on top of you?" Taya quipped with a wink.

The other two women laughed. Penny frowned. "He was most definitely *not* my high school crush—more like my enemy. And clearly, I should never have told the three of you about that. Now you'll hold it over my head for the rest of our lives."

"How long is he in town?"

"I just saw him again at the marina, and he says he's between jobs. But who knows what that means — he's been career obsessed ever since he left the island." Penny took a bite of the bread and enjoyed the soft, savoury flavour of the camembert as it flooded her mouth.

"You two sure are running into each other a lot," Bea said with a grin, then downed the last of her cocktail.

Penny rolled her eyes. "It was pure coincidence."

"How did he look?"

"He was shirtless."

"Oh, my." Bea laughed. "Is it getting hot in here?" She flapped the neckline of her shirt against her chest.

"He did look pretty good. I don't think he's been skipping arm day at the gym."

"You should ask him out," Taya said with a confident bob of her head.

"What? No. Definitely not. We drive each other crazy. And not in a good way. Besides, he's Rob's best friend, and you know he has a rule about his friends dating me. He was always going on about it when we were younger."

"You're not exactly a kid anymore. I don't think the same rules apply," Evie said.

"I don't know. He was pretty adamant about that one."

"Well, I don't know about any of you, but I've had enough of dating for a while." Bea sighed.

"Didn't you only go on one date?" Penny took another bite of bread.

Bea nodded. "And that was enough, apparently."

"So, Aidan's sticking to the whole idea of needing time with his daughter?" Taya asked.

"Unfortunately, yes. I get it, and I completely support him in wanting to do that. He's missed out on so much of her life —which was very unfair of her mother, in my opinion. But it's not up to me to get involved or to have a say. Aidan has enough to cope with—he doesn't need me horning in or getting my feelings hurt. And the truth is, I'm not upset at him. I'm upset at the situation — I want him to spend time with his daughter. I want them to have a connection. He's always longed for children of his own, although he doesn't often say much about it. And now that he has that chance, I'm not going to get in the way. I just hope there'll be room in his life for me at some stage."

Penny bit down on her lower lip. She felt an immense sadness for her friend, who seemed to have had a chance at happiness ripped away right when it looked as though things might work out. "Give him time. He'll come around."

"You're probably right," Bea agreed. "In the meantime, I've got a café to get up and running."

"Yes, you do," Evie added, her eyes glistening. "And it's going to be amazing."

"Thank you, my friend. I thought I should have a grand opening party. What do you say?"

"I say that's a great idea," Taya replied. "What can we do to help?"

Six

THE DAY dawned early and bright. By four thirty a.m., the sun crept above the horizon over the dark ocean and birds swanned about outside the cottage, diving for insects and waking the world with their calls. Beatrice had forgotten to pull the curtains shut on her bedroom windows and was woken by a shaft of sunlight spilling across the covers and over her face.

She squinted and blinked a few times before stumbling to the window to close the gap. But by then, it was too late to go back to sleep. She lay still, staring at the ceiling for a few minutes before reluctantly crawling from bed with a sigh. A glance in the bathroom mirror revealed dark smudges beneath her eyes and a sheet crease down one side of her face.

She grimaced and massaged the skin above her eyes for a few seconds before splashing cool water on her face. It'd been a hot night—she'd had to leave the overhead fan on so she didn't sweat through her fitted sheet. But now the humidity had lifted and the cool of the morning drifted in through the open windows, along with the shushing of the waves as they curled gently to shore.

She'd spent a restless night thinking about all the things that could possibly be wrong with her father's health. The worst-case scenario kept dinging around in her head with nowhere to go. She had to force herself to push those thoughts back down into the dark recesses of her mind.

He was going to be okay. There was no point getting alarmed yet — they were running tests. She could freak out once the results came back. But until then, she needed to think about something, anything, other than that. Thankfully, she had a full day of fun planned at Point Prospect to distract her.

By the time she'd taken her morning walk, showered and eaten breakfast, Bradford had pulled into the cove in one of his yachts. He anchored, then rowed a small tin boat to shore to meet her. She stood on the beach with a picnic basket slung over one arm, one hand up to block the glare of the sun from her eyes, and grinned.

When he reached the shore, she helped pull his tinny up on the sand, then gave him a hug. "The yacht is amazing. The others are going to love it."

He laughed. "It's fun to take it out for us to enjoy for a change rather than simply ferrying tourists out to the reef."

He helped her into the tinny, then motored back to the yacht. Bea smiled as she climbed aboard the yacht and got to work alongside Bradford as they set sail around the island. It'd been a long time since she'd been sailing. She'd competed as part of a club when she was young, and Dad had always taken them out in his small sailboat. But this yacht took sailing to a whole new level for her, and she couldn't wipe the grin from her face.

"I can't believe you do this for a living," she shouted above the noise of the wind in the sails.

Bradford looked the part behind the wheel, steering around the edge of the cove. He smirked. "It's a hard life, but someone has to live it."

Bea held her hat in place and sat at the front of the boat. She breathed deep of the sweet, fresh sea air and let all her worries ease out of her mind. She focused instead on the seagulls hovering overhead, the splash of salt water on her skin and the beautiful blue of the water as the yacht sliced through it.

When they approached Point Prospect, a large headland attached to a community with neighbourhoods, shops and a local surf life-saving club, Bea called Evie to find out where they were and discovered the rest of the group were waiting at the entrance to the beach. They anchored nearby and waved to their friends, and everyone hurried down to the beach to meet them.

The tinny motored to shore. Then Bradford ferried them all back to the yacht, and Bea helped set up a smorgasbord of picnic items and drinks in the galley. Aidan was there with his daughter. She offered him a smile and said hello to them both, but otherwise tried to stay out of their way. He'd asked for space, and she fully intended to give it to him although it was difficult, seeing him so close by with that smile tugging at the corners of his mouth in a way that set her heart racing.

They took turns swimming to the point, climbing the stairs and leaping off a rocky outcropping into the surging ocean below. Bea's heart was in her throat when she took her turn, but she'd done it a dozen times as a teen and knew the best way to land and how to swim away from the rocks. When her head plunged beneath the cold water, a thrill of adrenaline surged through her body, and she couldn't help laughing as her head broke through the water and into the sunlight.

When a modest pod of dolphins showed up, she swam alongside them, revelling in the beauty of the curious, intelligent creatures as they played around the swimmers. One of the dolphins eased slowly up to her, popped its head out of the water as if to greet her. She spoke to it, and it turned its head to the side so that one eye was fixed on her. Then it splashed its nose in the water, as though nodding. She laughed, and it ducked beneath the surface and swam away.

The dolphins didn't stay long, but the encounter was even more invigorating than Bea had remembered. The older she grew, the more she appreciated the chance to connect with nature.

It was good to be alive. And she felt very much alive in that moment.

Afterwards, she climbed back into the boat to dry off under the hot sun. Penny was there, talking to Rowan. Bea couldn't believe how much he'd changed since high school. He'd always been the tall, lanky, nerdy type. But he no longer wore glasses, he was athletic and tanned with a muscular physique, and even though there were a few strands of grey in his hair, he sported a thick head of it with luscious chestnut waves.

Penny clearly couldn't take her eyes off him, and the feelings seemed mutual from where Bea was sitting on a towel laid out on the deck beside a half-sleeping Taya. Evie read a book next to her, wearing an enormous straw hat and oversized sunglasses.

"Can you believe Penny?" Evie whispered, eyes still tilted towards her book.

"She seems very interested in Rowan, if that's what you're referring to."

"She's always had a thing for him. I don't know why she won't admit it," Taya murmured without moving.

"I don't think Rob's as thrilled with the idea as we are," Evie pointed out.

Bea looked for Penny's brother and found him standing to one side talking to Bradford, a beer in hand, his eyes drilling holes into the back of Rowan's head. He wore a snarling expression on his face.

"Oh, dear," Bea said. "Surely he can't still think he should have a say in who his sister dates."

"Maybe he knows Rowan too well and doesn't want her to be hurt," Taya offered, sitting up and adjusting her red bathing suit.

"I suppose that could be true." Bea's gaze had shifted to where Aidan was helping Grace into a snorkel and fins. He was already an attentive father. Bea had often thought he'd make a great dad. She was happy to see him finally getting to fulfil that role and knew how much it would mean to him. It brought tears to her eyes to watch them enjoying the day together. She might not be able to share the moment with them, but at least she was able to witness it.

At that moment, Penny screamed as Rowan threw her off the deck and into the ocean. She landed with a gigantic splash that soaked Aidan and Grace. Aidan shook his head, laughing, then helped Grace to climb down the ladder into the water below.

Penny came to the surface coughing and spluttering while Rowan leaned over the side of the boat to laugh at her. Rob glowered at them both, arms crossed.

When Penny climbed back onto the boat, she padded over to where Bea and the others sat. "Can you believe him? He threw me into the water like we're still teenagers. I could've broken a bone."

Bea laughed. "Hardly. It's only water."

"I wish someone would throw *me* into the water like a teenager," Evie muttered.

Penny frowned. "Huh?"

"Nothing. Hey, Pen, I have those photos Bea found in her cottage with me. Remember how you said some of them were from your family? Can you point them out again? I want to write down their names and maybe figure out the approximate date the pictures were taken. Bea helped me with it, but we want to make sure."

Penny sat beside her, wringing water from her ponytail. "Let me have another look."

Evie pulled the photos from her beach bag and held them up for Penny to see.

"Yep, that's my mother and my grandmother. This other photo has Dad in it."

"We think it was forty-five years ago or something like that because of when the cottage was built. But what do you think?"

Penny chewed on a fingernail. "That makes sense. I'm not in the photo, and I'm forty-five, but my mum was very young when she had me. So it must've been soon after this one was taken. She wasn't married to Dad yet, they were both still teenagers. But he was a friend of the family and used to go over there often in the summer holidays to fish and swim. His own parents worked on the mainland, so my grandmother took care of him."

"How young?" Bea asked.

"Sixteen."

"Wow, that *is* young. When did she get married?"

Penny shrugged. "Not until she was twenty-two. She married my step father — I call him Dad because he's the only father I've ever known."

"I forgot he was your stepdad," Bea said. "You mentioned it the last time we looked at these photos. I was going to ask you about it, but didn't want to pry."

"In my eyes, he's my Dad. I can't tell you who my actual father is, since Mum won't talk about him."

"She's never told you?" Taya asked, her brow furrowed.

"Nope. It's a family secret." Penny laughed. "I don't think I'll ever find out. Mum's determined to take it to her grave, my stepdad is clueless, and my grandparents are gone. No one else knows the truth."

Rowan emerged from the galley with a plate of food. He stepped over Penny's legs, and she scowled at him. Bea covered a laugh with one hand. The two of them were so cute together and obviously into each other, if Penny would push her angst aside for one moment and let herself feel the truth.

"Thanks for soaking me through," Penny muttered.

He lifted his sunglasses to peer at her. "Penelope, you look lovely today. Did I already tell you that?"

"My clothes are all wet and I can't find one earring. But thank you." Her tone was snide, but Bea could tell she was pleased even as she fingered the empty ear.

"I'm sure it will turn up." Rowan wandered off with a slow wink at Penny, whose cheeks flushed red.

"He's so full of himself," Penny said.

Bea bit down on her lower lip.

"With good reason," Taya added with a sigh as she lay back on her towel. "Did you see those abs?"

Penny grunted. "Who cares about his abs? He could at least *pretend* to be humble."

"I think he's just teasing you. He's not so bad," Bea said, lying on her back with her hands linked beneath her head. She stared up at the perfect, cloudless blue sky overhead. It was a beautiful day; she couldn't imagine any other way to make it better. Except, perhaps, if Aidan was beside her.

Seven

THE NEXT DAY, Bea was miserably sunburned. She'd applied suncream but hadn't reapplied often enough throughout the day, and now she was as red as a lobster on a buffet table.

She studied her back in the mirror, grimacing at the pain as she turned her head. There was nothing for it but to find some aloe vera to apply. Dad had plenty in his garden, which boasted an extensive collection of herbs and flowers. She could usually find whatever she needed for a natural remedy within his expansive grounds.

She threw on a light dress and an enormous straw hat to protect herself from the already glaring morning sun and padded up the hill to her father's large house. It looked like a sentinel staring out to sea as it guarded the island headland. Built of weathered timber, it was surrounded by maturing trees and shrubbery. Her father loved to putter around his garden and had a very effective green thumb — everything he grew flourished, while Bea's attempts always seemed to end in brown, limp plants and spindly trees.

Inside the house, the air-conditioning cooled her overheated skin, and she shut the door behind her, leaning against its smooth surface for a moment. Dad poked his head out of the kitchen, a tea towel slung over his shoulder.

"Good morning, love. Care for some pancakes?"

"Yes, please. That sounds delicious." She wandered into the kitchen, set her hat on the bench and poured herself a cup of coffee. "I got badly burned yesterday."

He glanced at her. "So you did. I've got plenty of aloe in Mum's garden."

"Thanks, Dad." He always called it Mum's garden, even though she'd been dead for over two decades. Bea's mother had planted it when Bea was a child. She had fond memories of traipsing through the strawberry patch, stuffing her mouth full of sweet, red berries. "I'll pick some now and then come back in to eat."

She went out the back and stuck to the shade along the side of the house as best she could. Any advance into the sunlight was painful on her shoulders. She should've left the hat on. Within minutes, she'd found the aloe plant, broken off a leaf and applied it to her skin. She collected a few more pieces and took them inside to put in a baggie to take home.

Dad set two plates of pancakes, along with fresh berries and yoghurt, on the table. She sat opposite him with her cup of coffee.

"This looks absolutely wonderful. You've become a real chef lately, Dad. Very impressive."

"Thanks, love. I was going to eat alone, but I'm very happy to have the company. It's been so nice having you live just down the hill. I assume you'll consider staying a while longer, now that you're opening the cafe."

She sliced off a piece of pancake and chewed. The freshness of the berries and the creamy yoghurt made her taste buds tingle. She swallowed. "I love it here. The cottage is perfect for me. I'm planning on sticking around indefinitely—I have no desire to go back to Sydney. I miss the kids, of course, but they're coming home as soon as the semester is over."

He smiled. "I'm looking forward to it."

"And how are you feeling, Dad?"

"Good," he said. "I thought I had a cold coming on yesterday but seem fine today. Why do you ask?" He studied her face, then his brow furrowed. "Oh, you've been speaking to your brother. Haven't you?"

She pushed a smile across her lips. "Sorry, Dad. He wanted me to know."

"It's not a big deal. I hope he told you that."

"He said you've been feeling dizzy and unwell for a while. I wish you'd said something."

"You've got enough on your plate without worrying about me."

"I like worrying about you, Dad." She squeezed his hand across the table.

"Well, I don't want you to fret. I'm sure it's nothing. It might be my blood sugar, or perhaps I'm dehydrated. My blood pressure was fine, so I don't think it's that."

"I know it could be nothing, but let's face whatever it is together. Okay?" Her stomach clenched even thinking about it. The idea that he might be sick, that something might tear them apart after they'd only recently reconnected, made her anxious. "I don't want..." She choked on a lump in her throat.

"What, honey?"

"I don't want to lose you. Not when I feel like I've only just found you after too many years away."

He shook his head, eyes glistening. "You're not going to lose me."

"You don't know that."

"Well, no one lives forever." His voice was soft and his eyes kind, but his words pierced her heart. She did know that; she knew it better than most. But she also knew she'd never recovered from her mother's death. How could she face another loss? Once again, she was getting ahead of herself. It was how she worked herself up into an anxious frenzy — by imagining things that didn't happen. It'd been something she'd struggled with ever since her mother's funeral. Images of that time flashed across her mind's eye — her father, pale faced and dressed all in black, leading Bradford by the hand through the cemetery; Bea's red-eyed reflection in the mirror as she steeled herself for the service while her heart pounded with pain in her chest.

Tears snaked down her cheeks.

"What's wrong, sweetie?" Dad's eyes narrowed with concern.

"Thinking about how you might be sick brings back memories of Mum's funeral."

Dad ran his fingers through his hair. "Don't go bringing all that back up again. We don't need to dredge old memories. We're okay, aren't we?"

"Yes, we're okay. I'm happy, really I am. But being on the island again, seeing you, fearing for your health, even spending time with Aidan and my friends — it's made me think about things I haven't pondered in decades. Most of all, Mum's death and what it meant to me and to all of us. How it changed the entire course of my life and the person I became —the daughter, wife and mother I've been. I still miss her."

She went into the kitchen to pour herself a glass of water. Dad followed and enveloped her in his arms. She cried against his shoulder.

"I'm sorry. I know it's silly. It happened so long ago."

"Not silly at all. I used to have a cry every now and then over her. I let myself grieve, and now I can remember the good times without it hurting that way anymore."

"I thought I'd moved on as well, but for some reason, it's coming back to the surface now."

"I suggest you let yourself face those feelings and deal with them." He wiped a tear from her cheek with his thumb, then kissed her forehead. "Let's finish eating."

They sat together and ate the rest of the pancakes. They talked about the café and the kids, anything other than his health or their past. By the time they were done, Bea was ready for a run on the beach. She told Dad goodbye and headed back to the cottage to change into a long-sleeved shirt and to apply sunscreen to her face and legs. Then she took off along the beach at a jog.

She rounded the end of the cove and jogged slowly along the beach that sat at the base of the cliff beneath her father's house. She made her way along the stretching golden expanse of sand beyond. The sun was glaringly hot and glanced off the sand like a bright light.

The depth of the pain in her gut shifted, as though a ball of emotion had been wedged there and was slowly unwinding as she ran.

"Beatrice, are you okay?" Aidan's concerned voice broke through her reverie. She could barely see, with the glare of the sun off the white sand in her eyes.

She pivoted to look for him. He stood near the water's edge in a wetsuit that was shucked to his waist. His muscular torso glistened with sea water as he set his surfboard down on the beach and walked towards her.

Tears threatened again at the sight of him. She missed him so much. All these years, she'd pushed her feelings for him beneath the surface. He'd left her — walked away when she needed him most. He didn't want her, and she'd had to move on with her life. But now she knew better — he'd been just as confused as she was, just as unsure of how to act or what to say. Keeping her distance now felt impossible.

She stumbled towards him and fell into his arms. She

pressed herself to his chest, feeling the saltwater seep through her running clothes.

"What is it? What's happened?"

She shook her head, unable to speak.

He studied her face a moment, one hand beneath her chin, then pulled her to him and wrapped his long arms around her. He held her tight until she felt as though she might have to gasp for air. She pressed an ear to his chest and listened to the steady rhythm of his heartbeat. It soothed her grief, and slowly she emerged from the pain of her sorrow into the bright, sunny day with the man she loved.

She knew that now. She loved him. Always had. It didn't take away from what she'd had with Preston — she'd loved him too, but this was different. With Aidan, it was a deep friendship built on a knowing. They'd spent so many of their formative years as friends before their dynamic changed to a romantic one. There was no one in the world who knew her better than he did back then. And in the end, she hadn't changed much. She was still that little girl he'd carried over the rocks when she'd cut her feet on oyster shells in the cove behind them. She was the girl he'd kissed right there on that beach for the very first time. She felt like a teenager all over again in his arms.

His voice was low, soft. "Tell me what's wrong."

"Dad's had a health scare, and it's making me recall Mum's death," she murmured.

A headache had begun to pound at the base of her skull.

Aidan pulled back and looked down into her eyes, his own dark with compassion. "Your dad is going to be okay."

"Do you really believe that?" She wanted it to be true. The adult she was now knew at some level that he was right, but the child inside couldn't let go of the fear.

"Yes, I do."

"You're right. Of course you are. I have to stay positive." She sniffled again and stepped back.

He caught her by the shoulders, his eyes ablaze. Then he raised a hand to cup the back of her neck and leaned down to kiss her. His lips coaxed hers apart, and warmth spread through her body. She forgot all about her tears and raised a hand to brush along his chiselled jawline. His lips were familiar, yet strange. Sensuous and yet like coming home all at the same time.

He took a step away from her with a pained look on his face. "Sorry, I shouldn't have done that..." He ran a hand over his hair, forming a row of spikes.

She blinked, stunned for a moment by what'd happened and by his words. Surely he couldn't believe their kiss was a mistake. It'd been everything she'd hoped for. More than she'd expected. It proved how he felt about her. What could keep them apart now?

He spun on his heel and strode away, picking up his surfboard as he went. He didn't look back. Not once. And she felt the pain of loss return as it throbbed in her chest.

Eight

THE NEXT DAY, Beatrice felt much better about everything. Regardless of the fact that Aidan had run off after kissing her, he *had* kissed her, and she was certain it meant more to him than he had let on. The cry she'd had seemed to have cleared out a deeply buried grief that'd been festering for years within the depths of her soul.

She felt lighter and happier than she had in a long time, and she wasn't going to let anything else get her down. It was a beautiful day, and she intended to enjoy it. Plus, there was plenty to keep her busy and to distract her from the fact that she had been dumped yet again.

She had a café to open and a party to plan, two things at which she thrived and that brought her an immense amount of joy. She threw herself into the preparations with gusto. One of the items on her to-do list she'd yet to take care of was to buy flowers for the grand opening event, and when she drove through Kellyville that morning, she'd noticed a florist shoved between a boutique dress shop and a Thai restaurant. So, she walked over from the café the first time she had a chance to place an order for native floral arrangements.

The florist was called *Betsy's Florals*, and it was a quaint little shop. A large picture window with a blue-painted trim showed a sneak peek of the arrangements available and the antique furniture scattered about the place. The shop was narrow and the walls were decorated with antique mirrors and framed local art, each with a price tag hanging from the bottom.

An elderly woman with wild grey curls stood behind a bench in the back of the shop, pushing tulips into a vase filled with greenery. Half-moon glasses perched on a pert nose, and fake eyelashes made black crescents on her cheeks. She was dressed in a brightly flamboyant flowing silk kaftan, and her fingernails were painted bright purple.

Beatrice walked over to meet her with a smile. "Good morning."

The woman looked up and grinned wide. "And to you, young lady."

Beatrice liked her already. "I need to order some flower arrangements for a party."

The woman set down the tulip in her hands and pushed her glasses back up her nose. "You've come to the right place, then." She had an American accent and drew out her vowels in a drawl. "What were you thinking of, honey?"

"Something native."

"We've got plenty of that around. I'll show you some photos, if you like. You just point out the ones you prefer." The woman handed her a loose-leaf binder with plastic-covered photographs of flower arrangements.

Bea flicked slowly through the pictures. "These are perfect. You make lovely arrangements."

"Well, thank you, honey. I love doing it. I guess that's the secret."

"I'm Beatrice Rushton, by the way. I've recently moved back to the island. I used to live here a long time ago."

"You're Elias's daughter, then." The woman's blue eyes sparkled.

"That's right — do you know him?"

"We see each other around from time to time. He's a lovely man."

Bea wondered if she'd stumbled across one of her father's girlfriends. She'd suspected he dated from time to time, but he never spoke of it openly and certainly didn't confirm any names.

"I'm Betsy, but I'm sure you guessed that from the sign outside. Betsy Norton."

"Pleased to meet you, Betsy." Bea held out a hand, and Betsy shook it. Her hand was warm and her handshake firm.

"Have you lived on the island long?" Bea asked.

Betsy shrugged. "Long enough, I guess."

Bea pointed to several flower arrangements in the book of photographs, and Betsy wrote up her order.

"I remember when you were a little girl," Betsy said suddenly. "You were such a sweet heart. Always walking around with that sweet crease between your eyes like you were thinking so hard about something."

"You were here then?"

"Yes, indeed. Although I wouldn't expect a teenaged girl to remember a middle-aged woman." Betsy laughed as she scratched the order into an old-fashioned ledger beside an antique cash register.

Bea studied a series of framed photographs that hung behind the counter. There was a young woman featured in every photograph — she was beautiful and dressed in a dancer's outfit with curled hair. The photos were in black and white, so it was difficult to tell what colour her hair might've been, but Bea liked to think it looked golden. Her toes were pointed, and she wore tights that showed off her lean, muscular legs.

"Is that you?" she asked.

Betsy glanced back over her shoulder. "Oh, yes, that's me. A long time ago. But it's amazing how quickly time passes us all by. I was that girl a moment ago, and now I'm me." She indicated herself with a wave of one hand.

"Is that the former Prime Minister with you?" Bea's eyes widened at the sight of Betsy standing close to a statesman from decades earlier. "And that... It couldn't be the Beatles, surely?"

Betsy arched an eyebrow. "I guess if it can't be, then it can't be."

"You knew the Beatles?"

"I met them. It was handy there was a camera at the ready to take the photograph."

Bea's gaze wandered across the rest of the photographs and realised that every single one contained someone famous or a dignitary. All except one photograph which was clearly more recent, in colour, and held a face very familiar to her — her father's. He held up a large silver tailor. The fish sparkled in the sunlight.

"Is that Dad?"

Betsy faced the photograph. "Your dad is a photogenic man. And let me tell you, he's one fine fisherman."

Bea didn't know what else to say. *How do you know Dad? What kind of relationship do you have?* But it seemed rude to pry, so instead she simply said, "Yes, he is."

"You know, honey, you have the prettiest eyes," Betsy said suddenly.

"Thank you."

"They're just like your mother's."

"You knew Mum?"

"Only in passing. She was a lovely lady, beautiful just like you."

"Dad says I look like her as well."

"You definitely do. You're about the age she was…" Betsy's voice trailed off, and her cheeks flushed pink.

"When she died? Yes, I know. I've been thinking about her a lot lately. Probably partly because of that, but also because I'm back on the island and memories are knocking on my door everywhere I turn."

Betsy finished up with the order and slammed the ledger shut with a flourish. "Memories have a habit of doing that, I'm afraid. But letting them in can be healing. Sometimes it's the very thing we need so we can move on."

"I think you're right about that." Bea sighed. "You should come to the party. It's on the date I gave you. It's the grand opening for my café, the one attached to Eveleigh's Books. It'll be fun, and of course the flowers will be divine. The food should be good too. I'm cooking."

Betsy's eyes twinkled. "Thank you. I'd love to."

Bea waved goodbye. As she walked out of the shop, Betsy called after her, but quietly so that Bea wasn't sure she'd heard exactly right.

"It was a travesty what happened to your mother. I'm sorry you went through all that, and so unnecessarily." Then Betsy turned and disappeared through a set of curtains into a room behind the counter.

Bea stood in silence, gaping after her. Mum had taken her own life. It was a tragedy for the entire family, but no one did it to her. What was Betsy talking about? It was as though she knew something Bea didn't, but there hadn't been any secrets, nothing hidden. They all knew what happened.

Mum had been unwell for a long time. She'd been anxious and paranoid and finally had taken a permanent step to remove herself from a situation she'd believed to be hopeless. None of them understood it, but the counsellor they'd seen at the time had told them that there was nothing they could've done. It was an illness, and there was no explanation that would suffice for them to understand her thinking. And that had been the end of it.

Bea studied the street, the way the sunlight glinted on the roof of the shop opposite, the scent of salt in the air, the sight of seagulls hopping along the pavement looking for scraps of food — it reminded her of hot summers, endless days swimming in the ocean, friendships that sustained her and the pain of losing a mother too young.

Coral Island was a place of joy, strength and peace for her, but it was also the setting for the biggest loss of her life. Another great loss had driven her back to it after she'd spent years avoiding having to face up to her past. But it was time for her to grow up. With one last glance over her shoulder she stepped out into the street, her shoulders squared with determination. Whatever Betsy was hinting at about her mother, she would uncover it — the fear she'd felt as a child at the prospect of discovering unwelcome truths no longer controlled her. She was ready to face it all.

Nine

THE AFTERNOON WAS BATHED in golden light. Penny paddled her surfboard away from the shore and dived beneath a wave. The swell was small, as it always was on the island, but she still loved to paddle out on her board and ride whatever she could catch. The water was cool on her skin, and the heat of the day had mellowed. The humidity had lifted, and in its place was a stunning sunset that lit up all the world in a rainbow of warm colours.

She sat on her board and pushed the hair from her face, legs dangling on either side. The water was crystal clear, and she peered down into it to watch a school of small fish darting one way, then the other. A parrotfish swam into view, its iridescent scales glinting blue then green then silver in the shifting light that filtered through the moving ocean waters.

The beach house looked dark above the dunes. It was surrounded by a lush garden that could do with a good day's worth of weeding, perhaps even a week — she didn't work as quickly as she used to these days. She much preferred to take her time and stop for a cold drink every now and then. But even though it looked a little unkempt, she loved the house. It reminded her of a happy childhood with parents who loved her. However, Beatrice's recent discovery of photographs in her cottage walls had thrown Penny into something of a state. Almost as though she was standing on quicksand. The happy childhood memories were shifting, and behind them, an ugly black monster reared its head.

She shuddered as the image sprang to mind for the second time that day. The murder of her grandmother was something she'd never fully processed. She'd been too young to really understand it at the time. But the event had shaped her childhood in ways she was only now beginning to understand.

The way that her stepfather had always been so protective of her mother. Her mother had never let her out of the house after dark. Had startled at every little noise. Penny had developed anxiety as a tween, and it was something she'd struggled with every day of her life since. Years of meditation had helped her manage it to the point where she had it under control — most of the time, anyway. But it'd still moulded her as a person and how she responded to the world around her.

She ran a finger over her lips. They were wet but chapped from so many days swimming in the ocean and not enough care. Much like the rest of her. These days, she'd stopped worrying about how she looked and had thrown herself into spending time in nature and taking care of the native animals on Coral Island. It was enough to keep her busy and was the kind of lifestyle that gave her satisfaction. The problem was, she'd come to realise that part of the reason she lived that way was to escape from the loneliness that'd descended over her like a scratchy wool blanket when her parents moved to the mainland and her last boyfriend left her.

After several long-term relationships that failed to result in a lifelong commitment, she'd found herself in her forties, childless and alone. Given the lack of dating options available on the island, instead of moving elsewhere or taking up a new hobby where she might meet people, she'd basically given up on the idea of finding *the one* and turned the beach house into a kind of hermitage.

The idea made her smile, and she shook her head. "Not funny," she whispered to herself even as her smile widened. Her sense of humour had always been a little off-kilter and self-deprecating, and it seemed to have grown worse in recent years. But if she couldn't laugh at herself, who could she laugh at? And she had to admit, laughing was better than crying.

She rode a wave partway to shore. It didn't take her far, but the Malibu board was built for ease of surfing, and she stepped back and forth up and down the board to ensure that it took her as far as possible. Then she paddled back to shore and perched on the sand, staring out at the water as the darkness crept across it. Watching the ocean was a kind of meditation, one she practiced often.

She pulled her wetsuit down to her waist. Her yellow string bikini had gotten twisted beneath it, and she reached around behind her back to fix it.

"What are you doing out here in the dark all alone?" Rowan's voice shocked her, and she almost screamed.

She slapped a hand to her chest and leapt to her feet. "You scared the life out of me. Why would you creep up on a woman in the dark like that?"

He laughed. "Sorry. I didn't realise you were so skittish."

"I've always been skittish."

"Noted," he said.

She wished she could see his eyes better. She could always tell what he was thinking by the look in his eyes, but the twilight made them darker than usual. He wore tailored shorts and a collared shirt. His feet were bare.

"What are you doing here?" she asked.

He shrugged. "That's a nice welcome. It's good to see you as well."

There was something so frustrating about the man. It was as if he tried to annoy her with every word he spoke. "I'm terribly sorry, Rowan. How lovely it is to see you on this fine evening. How can I help you?"

Her voice was laced with sarcasm, and she bent to retrieve her board from the sand before trudging back towards her house. He fell into step beside her.

"I'm not going to be around for too long, so I wanted to see you again. Is that okay?"

His words surprised her and momentarily rendered her mute.

"Oh."

He coughed. "Anyway, how's the wildlife refuge?"

She set her board down beside an outdoor shower on the side of her house and faced him. "It's good, I guess. We're running a little low on funding. I have this government grant I've got to apply for. But I never seem to have the time to sit down and do it."

"Instead of surfing?"

She laughed. "The ocean was calling."

"I can help, if you like. I've filled out a lot of paperwork in my time. I'm pretty good at writing mundane details into small boxes." He grinned. "I know focusing on one thing at a time is hard for you."

The outdoor light illuminated his face. His chin was covered with stubble in a way that was both adorable and completely out of character for him. He was usually so well-groomed that it was off-putting. The opposite of Penny, who hardly looked in a mirror most days.

The two of them were like magnetic poles. They didn't attract one another—they repelled. They couldn't be more different if they tried. And yet, there was something about Rowan that not only got under her skin, but intrigued her. She couldn't stand him, yet wondered what he was doing whenever he wasn't with her. The fact that she couldn't stop thinking about him infuriated her even more.

She rinsed off the board and herself while Rowan leaned against the house wall, arms crossed, watching her with a half grin on his handsome face. She was further irritated by his smugness.

"Why did you come over here to see me only to laugh at me?" she asked as she dripped dry outside the mudroom door.

His smile faded. Then he scowled. "I'm not laughing at you."

"Yes, you are. I've seen that look on your face for as long as I've known you. You enjoy criticising and teasing me. Why do you do it?"

He pushed his hands deep into his pockets. She opened the door. For the first time, the look on his face stopped her in her tracks. Had she gone too far?

His nostrils flared. "You wouldn't understand."

She'd been half joking, but his response made her frown. Did he really go out of his way to irritate and laugh at her? She'd wondered for years, but perhaps she'd been right all along. It must've been some kind of game for him.

"Try me," she said, pressing her hands to her hips.

He grunted. "You wouldn't understand what it's like to want something you can't have."

He raised a hand towards her face as if to cup her cheek with his palm, then let it fall to his side. His jaw clenched. Before she could respond, he spun on his heel and stalked into the darkness. The sound of his car door slamming and the engine revving to life before it growled away echoed through the quiet evening air. Penny gaped after him, her eyes wide.

* * *

After Penny had gotten dressed, she put off filling out the grant paperwork yet again and padded down the hallway in her bare feet to her brother's room. When he was on the island, he stayed with her at the beach house. But most of the time, he lived on the mainland, travelling around to whatever construction site he was working on at the time. He'd married a woman on the mainland five years earlier, but they were separated, so she'd seen a lot more of him lately than she had in a long time.

She knocked on his bedroom door, and it swung open. "You decent?"

"Come in, Pen."

She walked into the room and sat on his bed. The covers were wrinkled, and the pillow was at the wrong end. She'd never known Rob to make a bed in his entire life. He wasn't much good at picking up after himself, either.

"How are Jacqui and Julian?" His estranged wife and son lived in Townsville. Julian was five years old.

He sighed. "He starts school next week."

"That'll be exciting for him."

"I'm going to Townsville so I can be there to take him on the first day."

"That's good. You don't want to miss it."

He shook his head, his face grim. "I miss so much as it is."

"Do you think you and Jacqui will ever get back together?"

He sighed. "I hope so. I'm working on it. I've been calling her every day in the hopes that she'll talk to me, give me some idea what I can do to reconcile. But she's still not cooperating. She's good about Julian, though, and always gives me time to talk to him and tells me about what's coming up."

"If you really want to make things work, I'm sure you will."

"I don't know. She seems ready to move on. I think she might be dating again."

"What makes you say that?" Penny asked.

He chewed on his lower lip, eyes bright. "She said something about her mum coming over to watch Julian the other night. I don't know—the tone of it or something made me think she'd been on a date. But I could be wrong. I hope I am."

"You still love her?"

He shrugged. "I don't know anymore. All I know is that I miss having my family. I miss Julian and getting to be there with him when he wakes up in the morning. I don't have a residence, not a permanent one, so I can't have him come live with me, and it's killing me."

"Maybe it's time for a change of career?"

"You could be right. I'm getting too old for this business anyway. I've been thinking about settling somewhere and changing pace so Julian can stay with me during the holidays and on some weekends. He won't be a kid forever, and I'm missing it all." He brushed golden curls from his eyes.

"Your hair is getting too long," Penny said. She hated to see her brother in pain like this. It was hard to watch him suffer and not be able to do anything about it. She reached up to ruffle his hair.

He smirked. "Soon I'll be able to tuck it behind my ears like you do."

"Come into town with me tomorrow and I'll introduce you to my hairdresser."

He tugged a suitcase from beneath his bed and set it on the end of the covers, opening the lid. "I'm leaving, Pen. I won't be here tomorrow."

"That was sudden," she said.

"Not really, I got a call earlier about a job."

"I'm going to miss you."

He smiled at her as he shoved a pair of pants into a large canvas bag. "Me too. I'll miss you and this place. I've grown attached to having a swim every morning and lazing around on the sand. But the good times can't last forever. Time to get back to work, make some money."

"Speaking of unemployed bums lazing around on the sand, Rowan was just here."

"He was?" Rob glanced up at the door. "Why didn't he come in?"

"I don't know," Penny replied. "It was the strangest thing. He spoke to me for a few minutes, said something about wanting what he can't have, then marched off into the night. Do you have any idea what he was going on about?"

Rob's face clouded. He turned his back to reach for a bottle of water and shoved it into the side of his bag. "Stay away from him."

"Stay away from him? I hardly ever see him. What's going on, Rob?"

"I only have one rule—no friends dating my sister." His voice grew louder with every word.

Penny's brow furrowed, and she walked to the door, then faced him. "You do know I'm a grown adult?"

His eyes narrowed. "The rule still stands."

"I'm not your property or your wife. I'm your sister. I can date whoever I like."

"Not my friends, you can't. He's my best mate, and I don't want you anywhere near him."

"Why? Is he a criminal or a serial killer? If he's your best friend, surely you think he's a good person. Wouldn't that mean you'd be happy for me to date him?"

His mouth opened and shut like a goldfish. Finally, he exploded. "Stay away from Rowan Clements. I mean it, Penelope."

Anger roiled in her gut. How dare he presume to tell her

how to live her life. She was forty-five years old, for heaven's sake. She didn't need a chaperone or a babysitter, and she certainly didn't need an older brother acting like some kind of medieval father figure. "I refuse even to talk to you about this, Robert St James. You're not a teenager anymore, and I'm not a kid. Time to grow up!"

She stormed out of the room and down the hall, then slammed her bedroom door shut behind her so that a picture frame rattled against the wall. She threw herself down on the bed and hugged a pillow to her chest, her breathing ragged.

She didn't understand him when he got like that. He was a brute and a bully. She knew it was because he cared about her, but she didn't need his protection any longer. She wasn't the sweet, naïve little curly-haired girl he remembered from their childhood. She was a grown woman capable of making her own choices, and even he should be able to see that her choice wouldn't be to date Rowan Clements. They weren't suited to one another, and besides that, he lived in an entirely different country. It made no sense for Rob to be angry about something so unlikely.

Ten

BEATRICE WAS FLUSTERED. It was the day of the grand opening, and so far, everything that could go wrong *had* gone wrong. The paint the contractor had used on the walls turned out to be yellow when it was supposed to be white. They'd had to redo it the previous evening, it still stunk throughout as though the paint was wet. So, she'd had to open all the windows and run several industrial fans in the space to help air it out. Then the brand-new stove had failed to work, which turned out to be an electrical issue. The electrician was busy, then he broke his leg playing cricket and she had to find someone else to replace him last minute.

But finally, everything was in place. The paint didn't smell nearly as bad as it had, the white looked perfect against the stained timber floors, the stove worked, everything was ready, and the guests were due to arrive any moment.

Bea looked around her new café, her heart fluttering. What had she gotten herself into? It was so overwhelming, although she couldn't help being a little proud of herself for pulling it together despite the odds and in a very short time frame.

The outdoor area had the framing for vines to grow up the open walls. The plants were small now, but it wouldn't take them long to wind their way towards the ceiling. For now, the wires were laced with twinkle lights that would light up the entire area at night. The wrought iron tables and chairs she'd pictured in her mind's eye when she first looked at the space were dotted across the floor. Inside the café, the furnishings fitted the same coastal style theme as the outdoor area but instead of wrought iron, she'd chosen warm timber, chestnut leather, white walls and accents of blue.

"It looks amazing!" Evie stepped through the shared doorway to the bookshop, a black apron around her waist, her eyes wide. "You've done such a great job. It matches the bookshop perfectly and yet has its own style as well. I love it."

"Thanks," Bea replied. "And thank you again for agreeing to help wait tables. I still haven't found a full staff for the café, and I'm sure I'll be doing most of the work myself at first."

"Not a problem at all. It takes me back to my teen years. And I love a good reminisce." She laughed. "I'd better get back to the kitchen and make sure I have everything I need."

The guests had begun to line up outside, so with a quick intake of breath and a glance around the café to make sure everything was in place, Bea strode to the door and flung it open with a cry of welcome.

The event got underway, and Bea found herself fully occupied with conversation, refilling drinks, making coffees and helping Evie serve the trays of food she'd prepared ahead of time. She'd made finger foods, including macarons in various colours, small lamingtons, gem scones filled with jam and cream, tiny caramel tarts and mini cupcakes with delicate sugar flowers on top.

By the time an hour had passed, the anxiety was gone, and instead she longed to sit down and put up her aching feet. She'd been on them all day preparing for the opening, and now that the adrenaline had faded, her energy was going with it. But she pushed through, smiling and chatting with everyone as people came and went. The coffee she'd ordered from Brisbane was a big hit. She'd had to try a lot of suppliers before she found the perfect blend and was happy with it. It seemed her customers agreed, with several complimenting her and telling her they'd be back daily for more.

Finally the party was over, and people ambled for the exit as the sun set over the bay. Golden light filtered through the front door as Evie swept the floor. Bea cleaned the coffee maker then went throughout the café, setting upside-down chairs on top of tables. Betsy sat at one of the tables, looking through her purse as though she'd lost something. She stood and smiled at Bea, slinging her purse strap over her shoulder. She wore a long, flowing floral print dress, and her grey hair was curled neatly around her face. Her blue eyes sparkled.

"What a wonderful party and a lovely café. I know where I'll be coming to meet my friends for coffee from now on. That other place is so drab in comparison."

Bea's heart swelled. She'd been a little nervous that the island's residents might be resistant to change and loyal to their favourite haunts. She'd envisaged an opening where only her friends showed up, but it'd been nothing like that. Half of Kellyville must've sifted through the café at some point that afternoon, and she'd heard nothing but positive feedback so far.

"Thank you, Betsy. It's so lovely that you came."

"I wanted to bring you something, but I can't seem to locate it in the Bermuda Triangle that is my purse." She glared at the offending bag.

"Oh, well, thank you. I'm sure you'll locate it eventually."

"It was your mother's, and I can't for the life of me recall where I left it. I had it set out to bring to you." She shook her head in frustration.

"My mother's?" Bea couldn't imagine what Betsy was talking about. Her mother had died such a long time ago, and from what Betsy had told her the other day, they were only passing acquaintances. What would she have kept all these years, and why?

"Never mind. As soon as I figure out where I left it, I'll bring it right over. I know where you'll be." She laughed. "I don't know what's worse about getting older—the forgetfulness or the joint pain."

"I'm already forgetful, so it's going to be a nightmare for me," Bea said as she walked with Betsy to the door.

Betsy paused on the threshold. "Would you like to come fishing with me on Saturday morning? I've got a few hours to spare."

Bea wasn't usually the type to go fishing with people she'd only recently met. She was an introvert most of the time; it took a while for people to grow on her. But she already felt as though she knew Betsy. The woman's warmth seeped out of every pore. And besides, she knew something about Bea's mother — had kept an item belonging to her all these years. Plus, she was a friend of Bea's father. There was more to Betsy than Beatrice knew, and she was curious enough to push aside her normal discomfort and take the plunge.

"I'd love to go fishing. I'm sure Dad has a pole I can borrow."

"I'll pick you up around five."

"Right, five. AM or PM?"

"We can't wait until the sun has scorched the island—the fish won't bite then." Betsy winked. "It's the best time of the day. See you then!" She waved a hand over her shoulder as she grabbed the handrail and clacked on low heels down the front steps.

Bea tented a hand over her eyes and watched Betsy walk up

the street towards the florist's. She was about to step back inside the cafe when Aidan's voice stopped her.

"Hi, Bumble Bea." He stood behind her, hands pushed deep into his shorts' pockets. His hair was mussed, and he wore sunglasses. Her heart skipped a beat at the sight of him.

"I was surprised you didn't come to the opening," Bea said.

"I wasn't sure you'd want me there. Then on the way here, I got a flat tyre, so I suppose it was fate's way of telling me to stay away." He laughed.

She shrugged. "I don't know if I believe in fate. Not anymore."

"Really? Because you were always talking about it when we were kids."

"I thought it was a real thing, that everyone had a destiny that they would fulfil. That you were *the one* for me. That we'd fall in love, get married, have a family and live happily ever after. But now I know that's just a fairy tale. Real life isn't like that. You make your own fate."

He stepped towards her. "If you make your own fate, can you make it what you want it to be?"

"Of course," she replied. "But you can't control the decisions of others. Sometimes you have to accept that their fate isn't aligned with yours, and that can be hard." She wanted so badly to take his hand, to lean into his chest and reach for his lips with her own. But he'd made his choice—he didn't want to be with her. She couldn't control him any more than she could control the tide.

His jaw clenched, and he took another step towards her, his hands hanging by his sides. "I wish things could be different."

"But they can't." She pushed herself to smile even as her lower lip wobbled. She couldn't keep standing there looking at him, watching him step closer and closer. She was about to cry, and she wasn't the kind of woman who burst into tears for no reason. She was the calm one. The organised one. The one who pushed through the pain and made it to the other side without so much as a grunt. She'd even managed two labours without screaming or crying. She could handle a breakup with grace. She'd certainly done it before.

"I have to finish up in here."

He nodded. "Of course. I'm sorry I wasn't there. I really wanted to be." He raised his hands towards her, and she saw the black grease on his palms.

"You had a flat tyre—there's nothing you could do about it. I'm glad you're okay."

"Thanks."

"How's Grace?"

He cocked his head to one side and squinted at her. "Um... Let's just say teenaged girls are harder than I remembered."

Bea burst out laughing. She covered her mouth even as her cheeks warmed. "I'm sorry. I didn't mean to laugh."

He chuckled. "It's okay. I have to laugh myself—otherwise, I just might cry. I've never been a father before, and there's a reason you get a baby first — to break you into the whole thing. She's had a difficult time, and she seems to be taking it out on me. She's all over the place emotionally — one minute, she's laughing and joking with me, eating pizza. The next, she's yelling at me, crying and running to her room to slam the door. I'm left sitting there with a half-eaten piece of pizza hanging out of my mouth, wondering what on earth just happened."

Bea bit down on her lip to keep from smiling. Aidan was in pain, and even though the image he'd painted was a humorous one, she didn't need to add to his distress. She beckoned him into the café.

"Come in and sit down. I'll make you a coffee. Everything's better with coffee."

"Haven't you already cleaned the machine and shut it down?" he asked, following her inside.

She waved him off. "Never mind. It's easy enough to switch it back on again."

Evie had returned to her bookshop to close up, so they had the place to themselves. Aidan found a seat and took it off the table to set on the floor before lowering his lanky frame into it. Bea waited for the espresso machine to reheat and ground more beans in her coffee grinder. She made them each a coffee, then carried them to the table along with two leftover caramel tarts. She hadn't had a thing to eat all day, and her stomach grumbled in anticipation.

"These look amazing," Aidan said as she set the plate on the table in front of him.

"I hope so. They seemed to be popular at the party."

"I'll bet. No one around here has had anything this flash before. The locals are thrilled — curious, too."

She laughed. "They came through here wide-eyed, that's for sure. But I think they left happy."

"Good to hear. You deserve to be successful."

She blushed. "Thank you, Aidan. That means a lot."

"So, do you have any tips for me? After all, you've raised a teen girl."

"And I've been one too, if you recall."

His eyes sparkled. "I do remember that, vaguely."

She stirred sugar into her coffee. "It sounds like she's testing you. Will you love her only when she's nice and good, or will you still love her even when she's pushing you away?"

"That makes so much sense. Wow, I think you might be right about that." He ran fingers through his hair. "So, I should let her know somehow that I still care even when she's being difficult?"

"It's all part of parenting. Not accepting the bad

79

behaviour, but still making sure the child feels loved and accepted."

"Quite the balancing act," Aidan said as he took a sip of coffee. "Mmm... That's good."

"Thanks. I found it at this boutique roaster in Brissy. And yes, parenting a teen is a balancing act — like you're a juggler and you're on a unicycle making your way across a trapeze wire. Or something like that."

His eyes widened. "I don't know how you do it."

"*Did* it," she corrected. "Mine are grown and off living their best lives without me."

"The thing is, she's only got a few more years until she's an adult as well, and I don't want to miss a second of it."

"I don't blame you one bit." If she was in his position, she'd want to spend every moment and all of her attention on getting to know her child as well.

"Thank you. You've been so supportive throughout this whole thing. I feel overwhelmed most of the time, but I hope you'll still be my friend. I definitely need friends right now."

"Of course I will. Anything you need, just ask."

"Her mother, Kelly, is coming to visit."

"Wow. Really?" A part of her was anxious to meet this woman. She must be someone special. She'd captured Aidan's attention once. Would she do it again?

He nodded. "We speak regularly on the phone and have done ever since Grace first showed up. They had an argument and Grace simply ran off without saying a word about where she was going. Kelly threatened to call the police the first time I called. Then I explained to her that Grace came here without my knowledge and I would give her a place to stay until she's ready to go home. She calmed down after that. She thought I'd somehow gotten in touch with Grace and convinced her to leave. Now, she wants to see her daughter."

"I feel for her. She must've been scared to death when

Grace disappeared."

"According to Grace, her mother wasn't there — she'd gone to Melbourne for a few days with her new boyfriend."

"And she came home to an empty house."

"Yep."

"Wow." Bea shook her head. "I hope the visit goes okay. It sounds like it could get a bit heated."

Aidan gulped down another mouthful of coffee, then stood to his feet. "I've got to get going. I don't want to leave Grace alone for too long."

"Understandable," Bea said, following him to the door.

"Would you come and help me manage Kelly's visit? I think it would all go a bit smoother if you were there. You're so good with people, and you could help me deal with it all. I'm supposed to be cooking dinner for her in a few weeks' time. She's staying in town and coming over for the evening."

Bea's head spun. She wanted to be by his side during the hard times, but wasn't sure how her presence would improve what was likely to already be a volatile situation. Was it too much to expect of her, since they were taking time apart? She'd do the same for any one of her friends. And, if he wanted her there, she'd go. "I'm happy to come. How about I arrive early and cook dinner for you? That way, you can focus entirely on your daughter."

He sighed with relief. "Would you? That would be lifesaving. The only thing I know how to cook for guests is fish with slices of lemon."

As he walked away, Bea wondered why she'd signed up to help her ex-boyfriend entertain his ex-girlfriend. The tangled web was making her head spin. But he was also her friend and she cared about him and his relationship with his newly discovered daughter. If she could help ease some of his anxiety, she would. Besides, it gave her a chance to show off her culinary skills and size up Grace's mother.

Eleven

FIVE A.M. on a Saturday morning was inhuman. Bea rolled over in bed and slapped haphazardly at the bedside table to get the old-fashioned alarm clock to stop beeping. She groaned and covered her face with the end of her pillow. Why had she agreed to go fishing at the crack of dawn? Most sane people would be fast asleep in their beds for hours yet. Especially people who had just started a new business in their mid-forties and had every single muscle in their body aching. Those people deserved rest. They were *owed* rest.

With a sigh, she swung her feet over the edge of the bed and sat up, yawning immediately. If she didn't get up now, she'd go right back to sleep and wouldn't be ready for Betsy when she came. Still angry at herself for agreeing to do anything that involved her poor, bruised body being wakened so early on a weekend, she padded into the bathroom to splash cold water on her face. Instead of helping, that only made things worse. Now she was wet *and* aggravated.

She was dressed, but still sipping her first coffee in her travel mug when Betsy pulled up outside the cottage in her old pink panel van. Bea trudged through the yard with her father's fishing pole over one shoulder and his tackle box in the other hand. She yanked the van door open. It screeched, and she yawned as she climbed into the passenger seat.

"Good morning." Betsy was horribly chipper.

"Yeah." Bea waved a hand. She yawned again.

"Not a morning person?"

"Definitely not. And I'm sore all over from being in the café for three days straight. You know you're getting old when you work on your feet all day for the first time in decades — you feel every single moment of it in your body."

Betsy chuckled as she pushed the vehicle into gear and accelerated back up the hill. "Don't I know it."

"How do you do it?" Bea asked, smothering another yawn with her hand. "I feel like I need to sleep for a week."

Betsy shrugged. "You learn to give your body the rest it needs in the best ways that you can. If I have a busy day, I make sure to go to bed at a decent time."

Bea groaned.

Betsy only smiled as the car navigated through a bumpy patch of the track and onto the main road. "Are you ready to learn the location of my secret fishing hole?"

Bea shrugged. "I don't know. I suppose so."

Betsy gave her side-eye. "If I show you my fishing hole, you have to keep it secret. Those are the rules. I don't want a sudden onslaught of noisy young people descending on the place. It's nice and quiet, and that's the way I want it to stay."

"Me and my friends are hardly *young* people," Bea muttered.

"Oh, sweetheart, you have no idea." Betsy laughed. "You're still young, beautiful and strong. You should own that, honey. And don't ever tell yourself otherwise. Life's too short to be holding back affirmations for yourself. No one else's encouragement really matters in the end — oh, don't get me wrong. It's nice to receive it. But ultimately, only the words you speak over yourself will set you free."

Bea stared out the window, pondering. Betsy was right. In the end, it was Bea's inner voice she listened to for more hours of the day than she did anyone else's. It was her voice that pushed her to take a leap of faith or held her back from the edge. It was her own words of encouragement to keep going that had gotten her through the divorce.

They pulled up alongside the narrow, winding road and climbed out. They had to carry their fishing gear along an overgrown trail that was hard to see at times, but finally Betsy stopped and set her tackle box down beside a small cove.

She sighed. "Here we are."

"It's stunning," Bea said. "And so quiet."

The water lapped at a golden beach, and they were surrounded with tall black and brown cliffs that muted the sounds of the outside world. A few birds twittered and the low waves hushed along the shoreline, but otherwise, it was silent in that small world. The water was darker blue along the cliffs.

"It looks pretty deep there," Bea said, pointing.

Betsy nodded. "It gets deep fast. I've swum here many times in the summer months. And the sand drops away quickly, but it's a great place for a dip. No riptide, and the waves are small. You can lie on an inflatable raft and go to sleep."

"You know this from experience?"

"Let's just say, when I tipped off the raft and into the water, I got the fright of my life."

Bea laughed.

It only took a few minutes to set up their rods and to bait their hooks. And before long, the two of them stood side by side, knee-deep in the cool water, lines flung farther to sea.

"I've brought your father here a few times," Betsy announced suddenly, her voice soft.

She wasn't sure how to respond. She didn't want to pry, but she was curious. "The two of you are friends?"

"We've been friends for many years. Since before your mother died."

"You said you have something of hers?"

"Oh, yes. That's right." Betsy foraged in the pocket of her dress. "Here you go. I brought it to give to you, but then forgot all about it. I'd forget my head if it wasn't attached these days."

She handed Bea a small music box. It was made of silver, but tarnished, and it fit into the palm of her hand. She opened it, and a tiny plastic ballerina stood en pointe and began to twirl as tinny music echoed across the water. Images of her mother holding it up to the light in her bedroom, her laughter contagious as she spun around in circles like the little ballerina.

"Wow, I'd forgotten how beautiful it is. The carvings are so intricate."

"She carried that thing with her everywhere. I offered to give it to your dad once, but he said I should keep hold of it to give to you, since you'd always liked it. He didn't want to misplace it while he was waiting."

Bea ignored the gentle jab about her absent years. "How did you get hold of it?"

Betsy shrugged. "She dropped it. I was going to give it back to her the next time I saw her…"

"But you didn't see her again," Bea suggested, her heart constricting.

Betsy dipped her head in acknowledgement. "It was a difficult time for the entire island, but much worse for you and your family. If only she hadn't…" She inhaled a slow breath.

Bea could've finished the sentence for her. If only she hadn't done what she did. She'd had the thought herself a million times. Along with the question, *why* had she done it? Dad had explained to her years earlier that her mother was unwell and didn't see the world the same way the rest of the family did. But Bea had thought, in her young mind, that surely if they used the right words, they could convince her mother to see it all differently.

"I wish I'd said something," she whispered.

Betsy glanced her way. "You couldn't have changed the outcome. I've been alive long enough now to have learned a few things, and one of them is this—no one is able to change another person. We can encourage and love those around us, but we can't change them."

Bea's eyes watered. She tightened her grip on the fishing pole. "If I'd talked to her more, maybe she would've told me what was going on."

"And you wouldn't have been able to do anything about it. You were a kid, don't forget."

"But at least I might've understood."

Betsy shook her head. "You bear none of the fault. *I* could've done more." Her jaw clenched, and long grey curls danced in front of her sunglasses. "I saw what was happening, but I did nothing."

"What?" Bea turned her head and stared at Betsy. The older woman's profile was illuminated by brilliant, blinding sunshine.

"Nothing. Just the rantings of an old woman who wishes things had turned out differently. Don't mind me."

"What did you see?"

"Who knows? Now, let's hush or these fish will never bite."

There was clearly more than Betsy was willing to say, but Bea didn't want to push. The older woman had brought her here for a reason — perhaps that reason was to reveal something from the past. Or maybe she simply wanted to build some kind of relationship with Bea due to her own connection to Bea's father. It might be one of those things, both or none.

But pushing her wouldn't do any good. Bea could see that in the stubborn tilt of Betsy's head. She'd wait patiently, and Betsy would open up.

"Some things you understand better when you get a little older. I look back over my life, and there are things I'd have done differently if I understood the world the way I do now." Betsy wound in her line and cast it out again. "But there's no going back to fix anything. We have to live with our mistakes, move on and try not to make them again. It's all we can do."

"You're right about that," Bea admitted, thinking about her marriage and all the red flags she'd ignored while she and Preston were dating.

The time he'd yelled at her over a spilled glass of soda that'd ruined his shoes. Or the time he'd seen her walking home from the shops, both arms laden with shopping bags, and waved at her from across the street. They'd been engaged then, and he hadn't even stopped polishing his car to cross the road. She shook her head at the memory.

She should've known then he was selfish and wouldn't be the husband she needed him to be. But she was smitten — he was handsome, charismatic, fun and seemed to adore her. It'd taken her years to get over the immediate pain of losing her mother and then the loss of her relationship with Aidan. Preston had been a knight in shining armour, leading her back to a life of lighthearted, youthful fun again. And she'd relished those years as everything she'd needed and wanted in that moment.

"There were rumours going around the island back then, of course. Always were. But no one paid any mind to them. Your mother—she had things to say. People resented her saying what she did and wouldn't believe her. She was called crazy, unhinged, obsessed. They even talked about her needing help. But that was before it all went sour, of course."

"I didn't know that." Bea's brow furrowed. "People called

her names?" Her heart ached. Poor Mum. She'd been through so much. Bea had no idea that people on the island had treated her that way. She hadn't seen her mother in that light — to her, Mum had been a bright sun around which all the planets revolved. She was their centre, the place they all went when they needed a hug, a kiss on the cheek, someone to give them a word of encouragement.

There'd been the deep sadness at times that sunk her light into a black well. She'd go to bed and not come out of her room for days on end. But when she did emerge, the darkness lifted and the light returned. Bea learned to appreciate those days — when all was right with the world. The entire family's moods shifted and swayed around her mother's highs and lows. Looking back, she could see how unhealthy it had been for them all, but at the time, it'd been normal to her. Wasn't everyone's mother like that? Now she knew better.

They fished in silence for another half an hour. The water lapped peacefully around Bea's legs. A light breeze picked up as the morning wore on. Then a bright splash of colour at the top of the cliffs caught Bea's attention. She looked up, one hand over her eyes to cut the glare, and saw a teenaged girl carefully climbing down a crooked path.

"Who is that?" Betsy glanced up even as a fish leapt from the water on the end of her line. "Oh, look out — I caught one. A nice-sized parrotfish. Looks like I'll be eating well tonight."

While Betsy was preoccupied with reeling in her fish and taking the hook from its mouth, Bea watched the girl make her way down the side of the cliff. When she drew closer to the beach, she recognised her as Aidan's daughter. Grace Allen wore ripped denim shorts and a loose aqua crop top that showed off her flat, tanned stomach. Long, golden hair partially obscured her face. She hadn't seen Bea or Betsy yet. And when she disappeared behind a rocky outcropping, Bea didn't see her again. She must've settled down behind the rocks somewhere.

"I'll be right back," Bea said, pulling in her line and setting her rod in the sand.

She trudged along the beach and then climbed the black rocks, cutting one toe on an exposed oyster shell. She grimaced with the pain. She'd have to apply antiseptic cream when she got back home or it could get infected. She used to run across rocks like these when she was a kid, never getting hurt, but she was out of practice.

At the top of the rock, puffing lightly, she glanced over to find a small cavern-like space with sand at the bottom and an overhang. Jutting out from beneath the overhang was a pair of long brown legs and bare feet. It was Grace, and she'd clearly found a hideaway for herself — somewhere to go where no one would find her.

With a smile, Bea backed down the rock and walked along the beach away from the girl. She wouldn't be the one to spoil her secret or impinge on her quiet. She returned to Betsy, and they fished a while longer. They talked about her father, about Bradford and his girlfriend. Betsy seemed to know far more about Bea's own family members than she did. They discussed life on the island and what it was like for Betsy to move there from the United States so many years ago.

"Your accent is still fairly strong," Bea said as they packed away their fishing gear. They'd each caught two fish and had them gutted in a small esky to take home with them for dinner.

Betsy laughed. "Not nearly as strong as it was. I'm told it gets worse when I call home. But most of the time, I have a mixture. Half American, half Australian."

"Would you ever move back there?"

"No, this is home now. I raised my child here. I buried my

husband here. My friends and business are on the island. I have nowhere else to go."

Bea considered her words. She couldn't imagine moving to the other side of the world and putting down roots. It must've been difficult at first, but Betsy had built a life for herself and seemed happy. Bea had done something similar when she moved to Sydney. She hadn't known anyone there and it had taken a while to feel at home in the big, bustling city after her quiet, relaxed life on Coral Island. But now she was home again, she wondered how she'd ever managed it, how she'd ever believed herself to belong there. This was her home and she had no plans to leave again.

Twelve

PENNY LEANED her head towards her chest and squeezed the back of her neck with one hand. It ached from sitting at a desk all day staring at a screen. Paperwork was a necessary part of running the wildlife refuge, but it wasn't one of her favourite tasks. She preferred being out with the animals. Still, she couldn't do that unless she paid the bills, and that was getting more and more difficult.

She'd done her best to juggle the minimal resources remaining in her bank account and hoped it was enough to get her through the next thirty days. After that, she'd have to come up with some other kind of plan. She still hadn't heard back about the government grant she'd applied for, and the refuge was well and truly skint.

With a yawn, she got to her feet and stretched her arms over her head. She stretched her neck to one side, then the other, and wandered out through the door to check on the animals in the outdoor enclosures. It was her favourite time of the day — afternoon, before the sun had begun its descent beyond the mainland. The animals needed to be fed, and many of the creatures who were nocturnal, sleeping through the daylight hours, began to stir and come out of their hiding places. She could talk to them, pat them, spend time watching them frolic and eat.

She fed the kangaroos first, then cut up vegetables for the wombats. She was the only one on duty that afternoon, so she had to undertake the entire afternoon feeding schedule on her own. It wasn't a large sanctuary, so it was manageable. But she was glad the reptiles had already been taken care of by the morning crew or she might not be able to get it all done.

When she walked into the wombat enclosure with the tray of sliced vegetables, she noticed a shadow against the outer fence. The shadow followed her as she went, then stopped by the wombat burrow when she did. She pushed half of the vegetables into the feeding trough with one finger, then spun around to stare at the shadow against the fence. A small brown eye looked at her through a gap between palings. It blinked.

"Hi," Penny said.

There was no response. She walked closer. The shadow backed away.

"Do you like wombats? They're one of my favourites. I love how they curl into a ball to go to sleep. Don't you?"

The shadow slowly drew close to the fence palings, and the brown eye reappeared. "Yes," a small voice said.

"Would you like to feed them?"

Penny went to the front gate and found a small girl standing there who looked to be around eight years old.

"I'm Penny." She smiled.

The girl chewed her lower lip. "I'm Sam."

"Nice to meet you, Sam. Are your parents okay with you coming into the sanctuary to feed the wombats? Maybe I should call them."

"They're not home," Sam walked through the gate.

"Okay." Penny shut the gate behind her after checking there was no one else around. Why was this girl standing outside the sanctuary by herself? The closest houses were only a few blocks away. Perhaps she'd wandered over alone. Or maybe someone was nearby. Either way, she hoped the girl knew a phone number to call although these days, few people memorised numbers since everything was on speed dial.

The girl followed her to the wombat enclosure, and Penny helped her feed them the rest of the vegetables. Her hair was tangled, her clothing ratty and stained. She had bare feet, and her knees were covered in half-healed scabs.

"Are you here with someone?"

The girl shrugged. "Dad's busy."

"Oh, I guess that makes sense. Do you live near here?"

A nod.

"Does your dad know where you are?"

"He's at work."

"Are you hungry?"

Her brown eyes found Penny's. She nodded again.

"Well, come on, then. I've got some cake I was about to cut up for afternoon tea. It's red velvet with cream cheese icing, my favourite. I'm starving myself. I hope you are too. Someone has to eat the cake. I'd hate for it to go to waste. And since my brother isn't here, it will have to be the two of us."

After cake and chocolate milk, coffee for Penny, the little girl wandered back in the direction of home. Penny offered to drive her, but she said she'd rather walk and something about not being allowed to get into a car with strangers.

Inside the refuge, she finished up for the night, locked everything, set the alarm and then left via the gate for the short walk to her beach house. She showered and put on a loose-fitting spaghetti-strap floral dress. As she towelled her hair, she wandered into the kitchen and studied the photographs strewn across the kitchen table.

Evie had given her a copy of the old photographs Bea found in her cottage walls. The beach house was featured so prominently in many of the images that Evie thought she might like to enlarge some of them to hang on the wall. The house looked new and fresh. Now it was sagging and filled with memories.

She poured herself a glass of water and sipped it while she flicked through the photographs. There was one in particular that showed the beach house in profile in a good light. That might do to hang on the wall in the entry. She loved that it was black and white. The retro look would work well with the décor in the place, since most of it was almost as old.

There was a knock on the front door, and she hung her towel over one of the chairs and hurried to answer it. Rowan smiled at her as he leaned against the doorframe, towering over her.

"Hi," she said.

He straightened. "Want to go for a swim?"

"I just showered," she said, touching her still-wet hair.

"Oh." He looked confused for a moment.

"Come in. I'll make a cup of tea."

Another smile. "Okay, sure."

He followed her to the kitchen, then sprawled across a chair in a way only confident men manage without falling to the ground. It made her want to slap him or laugh at him or kiss him very hard on the mouth. She wasn't sure exactly which would come first, but it provoked her in a way that only he could manage. The fact that he bothered her so much hadn't escaped her attention. In fact, she'd thought about it constantly ever since his return to the island. But she still couldn't understand it.

Bea was right about him. He wasn't so bad — in fact, he

could be downright thoughtful at times. And he'd been a good friend to her brother over the years. Rob had admitted as much many times. He was handsome and athletic, two things she very much appreciated in a man. And he did have perfect abs. But that grin — perhaps that was it. His grin was so provocative. And his eyes. He looked at her as though he might devour her at any moment, like she was a delicious piece of his favourite cake. And the smile said he wouldn't feel one bit bad about it. That had to be the reason her temperature rose around him and her stomach did flips.

No doubt he was looking at her like that while he sat at her kitchen table, but she wouldn't give him the satisfaction of noticing. Instead, she busied herself filling the kettle with water and setting it to boil, then cutting another slice of the red velvet cake that she'd brought back from the wildlife refuge with her after Sam devoured three pieces. She'd have to remember to take some more substantial food with her tomorrow in case the girl showed up again. It was clear she was ravenous, the poor little thing. Never having had children of her own, she wasn't entirely sure how much they should eat at that age, but Sam's hunger seemed out of step with her size.

Expecting Rowan's eyes to be on her, his smile lazy and suggestive, she spun in place, her cheeks warm, but instead found him staring at the photographs splayed over the table.

"What are you doing with these?" He glanced up at her, his green eyes darker than usual.

"Evie thought I might like to keep them, since they're of my beach house, and this place is part of my heritage. I'm the only one in the family still living on Coral Island."

"I wasn't expecting to see photos of my family here, that's all..."

Penny set the plate of cake on the table in front of him. "Yes, of course. Sorry, I didn't think about it, but I'll make sure to get you a copy if you like. Do you have many from back then?"

"No, none really. My parents didn't take many photos. Although now I'm seeing these, I wonder who the photographer was, since both parents are in the images. And yours are too."

Penny studied one of the photos. "You're right. Who could've taken them?"

"Maybe it was a neighbour."

"Maybe... Do you see your stepdad anymore?" She wanted to find out everything about this man who kept showing up in her life. She was ashamed to admit that as long as she'd known him, she'd never really asked him much about himself. He was a mystery to her.

She poured two cups of tea and put one in front of him.

"Thanks," he said, picking up a piece of cake and taking a bite. "Wow, this is delicious. You're a really good cook."

"You sound surprised."

He took another bite. "I'm going to have to come over here more often."

She sipped her tea, revelling in his enjoyment. Nothing made her happier than bringing another person joy. Except maybe taking care of animals. It was a close race — bringing joy to humans and animals were the two things she loved most.

"In answer to your question, no I don't ever see my step-dad. And I don't want to. My dad left before I was even born. Mum told him she was pregnant, and he took off. They weren't married, and she was very young. But then she met my stepdad, Buck. He was good to her and promised to take care of her. She was scared of the future. Her parents weren't happy she was pregnant, but they fully intended to let her live at home and bring the baby up there. But then her father died, and her mother couldn't pay the bills. They knew they'd have to sell the beach house and that's when Penny's family bought it. At least, that's what Mum always said. So, she married my stepdad to have some stability for me when I was born. Of course, it turned out to be a complete disaster, and she finally had to divorce him."

"Wow, that's horrible. I'm sorry that happened to you and your family. That must be what these photos were about — the beach house passing from your family to Penny's?"

"Probably. After Buck left, things got a lot better. Mum has her bakery and café, and she seems fine. She's not the same person she was when I was little—things happen that change us, I suppose. But she's living her life, and at least she's not under his thumb anymore."

"You said he still lives on the island?"

"That was the last I heard. He was living in a cabin on the other side of Blue Shoal. There are a few houses around Amity Point, and his is one of them. He's a bit of a hermit these days and lives off his fishing and garden, I believe. But I have no desire to see him again. He ruined our lives for so many years. When he left, that was it for me. I haven't seen him in a long time."

"Totally understandable," Penny replied, her heart aching for what Rowan and his mother went through. It was hard for her to believe that had been his life when she'd known him all those years ago. He'd always seemed so upbeat and fun. She'd mistakenly believed he had everything going for him — he was clever, an athlete, he loved to surf and was good at it, plus he was handsome in a very typical way. He'd joked with his peers and built a reputation as one of the popular boys. Yet he'd hidden so much pain and personal strife from the world around him.

"So, if you want me to make copies of the photos, I can. Not this one, of course." She pushed aside the photo with his stepfather in it. "But these other ones are really nice."

"That would be great. Thanks. You're always so thoughtful."

Suddenly it felt awkward again. The room small, his presence so large in it. "Happy to help."

"Speaking of help, I came by to see if you still need help with the government grant application. Anything else you need to do?"

"Not right now. I haven't heard back. But if I get the grant, I'll have a lot of paperwork to complete."

"Give me a call and I'll come over."

She was pleasantly surprised by his enthusiasm. But the truth was, she'd need all the help she could get. If the grant didn't come through, she had no idea what she'd do to keep the refuge running. There was no point in worrying about something she couldn't control, but she'd need to come up with a plan soon if she was going to make it work.

Thirteen

IT WAS A BEAUTIFUL DAY. Autumn had arrived and with it, some slightly cooler weather. Bea loved autumn and winter on the island. The sun wasn't as relentless, there was a slight chill in the air overnight, and the ocean had a more deeply blue tint rather than the glaring brilliance of summer.

She climbed out of bed with a smile on her face, pushed her feet into her slippers and padded into the kitchen to make herself a fruit salad with yoghurt for breakfast, along with a giant mug of cappuccino from the lovely espresso machine Aidan had bought her.

Not only was it autumn, but it was the first Sunday of the university break, and she expected both of her children on the afternoon ferry. It was the first time the two of them would visit her cottage together, and she was more excited than she'd thought possible. She couldn't stop smiling as she made coffee, then carried everything out onto the back verandah to sit looking out across the beach as she ate.

She spent the day getting chores done around the cottage. After a full week in the café, she was exhausted, but happy. She'd had customers every single day, and some were becoming regulars. She'd found a couple of high school students to help after school and on weekends, which was how she was able to take the day off to prepare for her children to visit. She did the laundry and tidied, cleaned and scrubbed. She even took an hour to lie in the bathtub with a mud mask on her face and a pillow under her neck while she listened to an audiobook.

Finally, it was time to collect them from the ferry. She hurried to the car and picked up Dad on the way there. He must've been excited, but didn't show it. His entire face was passive. Only his grey moustache twitched as though he wanted to laugh or smile, but was holding it in.

"You looking forward to seeing them?" Bea asked.

"Can't wait."

She smiled to herself. He'd always been stoic, but she could read his emotions after years of practice. The way he folded his hands in his lap as she drove showed he was tense. He stared out the car window at the landscape and didn't speak — that meant he was thinking, anticipating seeing the kids again. She wondered if he'd heard anything back about his medical tests yet. He might not tell any of them if the news was bad. She'd have to ask him if he didn't say something soon, although she knew how much he hated anyone to prod for information.

"There they are." She pulled into the parking lot to see the ferry already docked. Harry and Danita walked across the tarmac with bags slung over their shoulders. Dani waved a hand at the old station wagon as Bea parked.

Danita's blonde hair shone brilliant under the heat of the sun, her fedora tipped forwards over dark sunglasses. Harry's peaked cap had a mass of brown curls protruding beneath it and his lanky frame ambled towards her, shoulders slightly hunched.

She climbed out and ran to throw her arms around first Dani and then Harry, who lagged behind. She kissed his cheek.

"Finally! You're on the island. I can't wait to show you around."

He smiled through a grimace. "I've been here before, Mum."

"I know, but I was visiting then. Now it's home and you haven't seen the renovated cottage."

"It's good to see you, Mum," Dani piped up as she threw her bag into the boot of the car. "I feel like I'm home as well."

Her words warmed Bea's heart. She'd been afraid the children wouldn't cope with her selling their childhood home in Sydney. That spending holidays on the island or with their father in Melbourne would make them feel ill at ease, as though they had no roots. But so far, they seemed relaxed about the change in their family's circumstances.

As she drove back to her father's house, Dani and Harry took turns talking. They chattered about everything going on in their lives, at university, with their friends. Harry had joined the university soccer team. Dani was loving her new area of study. She'd made friends with a large group of girls who socialised together on the weekends. Plus, she'd found a job at a local café and was keen to use her newfound skills to help Bea over the holidays.

"I can't believe you have your own business, Mum." Harry studied her reflection in the rearview mirror. "And you're so tanned and fit. It's like you're a whole different person."

"I had my own business in Sydney, if you recall." Sometimes she wondered how much attention her children had paid to the life she lived when they were young.

He grunted. "Oh, yeah. That's right. But it wasn't the same thing."

"No, that's true. I have to be on my feet all day long now, serving customers. It's taking me a bit of getting used to. I'm definitely feeling fitter and stronger after the renovations and now the café, but I'm also exhausted all the time. I've been falling asleep in my armchair at nine o'clock every night." She laughed. "Just like Pa."

Her father quirked an eyebrow. "Hey now, don't bring me into it."

"Never mind, Dad. You're fit as a fiddle. Only you like a good sleep in your armchair—there's no denying it."

"True enough," he admitted. "Although it's the gardening that takes it out of me. That and my spearfishing."

"Did I tell you I went fishing with Betsy Norton yesterday?"

His eyes narrowed. "No, you didn't mention it. I wasn't aware the two of you knew each other."

"She gave me a music box Mum dropped years ago. Said you told her to hang on to it to give to me, since I'd appreciate it more. Does that ring a bell?"

He sighed. "Oh, yeah. I forgot about that."

"Mum loved that thing and carried it in her pocket. She used to pull it out and stare at it going around and around. The music drove the rest of us batty."

Dad laughed. "Yes, it did. I'm glad Betsy kept it all this time. I didn't want it—too many memories. And besides, I'd probably have lost it long ago."

"It was very kind of her. We had fun together."

"That's good." Dad fell silent, his brow furrowed. Bea wondered how he felt about her getting to know Betsy and what his relationship was with the florist. But she didn't want to pry. If he cared to tell her, he would.

The kids were busily talking to each other in the back seat as Bea parked in front of Dad's house, updating one another on their semester, their results and how hard their assignments had been. Comparing notes.

"I can't believe you're back in first year," Harry said. "Just like me. I'm going to graduate at the same time as you."

Dani rolled her eyes. "I'm far more experienced than you,

though, since I've already done two years of study."

"It doesn't matter. You'll be graduating in four years, just like me."

"You still have ages to go if you study medicine."

Harry shrugged as he climbed out of the car. "That's true. But we'll graduate undergrad together."

"Maybe we can wear matching robes," Dani said.

He laughed. "I think they make you wear specific ones depending on what you study."

"You're no fun," Dani quipped.

They walked into the house without their luggage. They'd be staying at the cottage, but Bea thought they might like to eat dinner with their grandfather in the big house on the point before heading down.

Bradford was there, waiting for them in the kitchen. He was slicing tomatoes when they walked in. He hugged both the kids and then carried a bowl of fresh salsa with a plate of corn chips out to the back deck.

"Let's sit outside," he said. "It's such a beautiful evening."

When they were all seated, Bea dipped a chip in the salsa and ate. The fresh taste of cilantro, tomatoes and onions filled her mouth and delighted her taste buds. "I can't believe you made fresh salsa. What has happened to you, brother?"

He sat opposite her with a bottle of beer. "I'm domesticated these days."

"You'll make someone a fine husband one day."

He threw his head back and laughed. "I think I blew my chance at that."

"I'm sure you'll get another shot." Dani filled a plate with chips and salsa. "This is amazing, Uncle Brad."

Bea got everyone a drink and sat again. The cool evening breeze lifted her hair from her sweaty neck. She looked out at the setting sun and listened to the cacophony of birds as they settled in the trees around the property for the night.

"I love it here," she said.

Harry spoke around a mouthful of chips. "It's the best. Can we go snorkelling tomorrow?"

"Maybe not tomorrow," Bea replied, "but soon."

Dad joined them on the deck, his face pinched. He sat with a glass of water and stared down at his hands.

Bea leaned forward. "What's wrong, Dad?"

He looked up at her, his eyebrows drawn together. "I got my test results back."

Bea's stomach churned, and her heart rate accelerated. "What did the doctor say?"

"I have to go in tomorrow to talk about it, but it looks like I may have had a stroke."

His words sucked the air from Bea's lungs. Everyone fell silent. After a pause, Bradford spoke first.

"It's going to be okay, Dad. You're a fighter."

Dad offered him a wan smile. "You're right, of course. And it was a mild one, obviously."

"We'll all help," Bea said, reaching for his hand to squeeze it even as her eyes filled with tears. "Whatever you need. I can't believe we didn't know."

"I had my suspicions. But I seemed to recover, so I thought maybe I was wrong." Dad ran a hand through his grey hair, standing it on end. "They're concerned I might have another one, a worse one, so there'll be medication."

"That's good — I mean, that they have something you can take," Dani said, her voice small.

Dad offered both children a look of confidence. "They'll take care of it—don't you worry. I'm going to be just fine."

But Bea knew his words echoed hollow because his hands were clenched into fists, one around her own. He'd stay strong; she knew him well enough to understand that. But she was afraid. She didn't want to lose him or for him to suffer long-term health complications. Anxiety fluttered in her chest.

Fourteen

THE ISSUE of bills sat heavy on Penny's mind. Bills to pay. Bills on her desk at home. Bills in her email inbox. Running an animal refuge was expensive, and she still hadn't heard back about the government grant. She should've applied for it months earlier, but she'd been so busy. And now, the process was slow, and she would fall behind on her payments and who knew what might happen? Once again, she cursed her own lack of organisational skills. If only she had someone else to do the things she was terrible at managing.

She turned the wheel of the car, downshifted to go up a rise and then coasted along the downhill slope past a neighbourhood of small, squat homes. Up ahead, a girl played in the dirt on the side of the road. Her long brown unkempt hair gave her away. It was Sam, the little girl who'd helped feed the wombats a few days earlier. She was all alone again, and a little too close to a road for Penny's comfort.

She pulled over and climbed out. The heat of midmorning was like a slap in the face as she walked through the wispy sea grass and sand to where Sam stood, peering at her like she knew she was in trouble.

"I stayed home sick," Sam said, her eyes darting from Penny's face to the ground and back again.

"I hope you feel better soon." Penny crossed her arms over her chest. "Where's your dad?"

"Work."

"Who's taking care of you?"

The girl didn't answer.

"Where do you live?"

She pointed over her shoulder at the neighbourhood behind them.

"Come on. I'll take you home and we can call your father."

She followed Penny to the car and climbed inside. The air-conditioning was a welcome relief. Penny leaned back, eyes closed for a moment to soak it in.

"Don't call Dad. He's busy. He says not to call him at work because he can't take time off to talk."

"Fine. We don't have to call him if you don't want me to."

She started the car and followed Sam's directions to a small fibreboard house with chipped paint and a red tile roof. Sam leapt from the car as soon as it was parked in the driveway.

Penny stepped out of the car, leaving the door ajar. "Are you okay now?"

Sam nodded. "I take good care of myself."

"I'm sure you do, but here. I'm going to give you my phone number just in case you need to call someone for help. We all need help sometimes."

She scrounged around in the car to find a piece of paper and ended up with a petrol receipt. Then a working pen — there was one in the glove box. She wrote her phone number on the receipt and handed it to Sam. "Call me if you need anything, okay? I'm usually just down the road at the refuge. I wrote my full name down on the paper too, Penelope St James, so you can show your dad and let him know you spoke to me."

Sam smiled for the first time. "Okay. My name's Samantha Norton."

"Norton? Do you know Betsy Norton? She runs the flower shop in Kellyville."

Sam squinted, her nose wrinkled. "No. I don't know anyone by that name."

"Oh, okay, just a coincidence then, I suppose. I'll see you later, Samantha Norton."

Penny waved goodbye as the car pulled out of the driveway, then waited to make sure the girl went inside the house. Her heart was troubled. No doubt Sam's father was doing the best he could to take care of his daughter and work at the same time, but someone should be looking out for her when he couldn't do it. Besides that, Sam's hair was knotted and greasy, her face dirty, her clothes too small and stained. She wished there was something she could do to help without overstepping.

If she could get in touch with Sam's father, perhaps she could offer to help the girl. But how to phrase the offer without offending or appearing to be a stalker? She still didn't know where Sam's mother might be — although from what the girl had told her, it didn't seem like she was still in Sam's life, for whatever reason.

With a brief pause at the intersection, she turned onto the main road and headed for Kellyville. She was meeting Bea and Evie at the café. Perhaps they'd have advice about what she should do.

* * *

The smell of coffee and baked goods greeted Penny as soon as she stepped through the retro timber-and-glass front door of the café. A bell tinkled overhead, and she smiled as Bea hurried to greet her. She kissed her cheek, a tray balanced on one hand.

"I'll be right with you just as soon as I've served the table outside."

"Good to see you!" she called after Bea.

Evie was already seated at a small round table near the back of the café. She was reading a book, but put it down as soon as Penny sat.

"There you are," Evie declared with a grin. "I'm looking for a book for next month's book club selection. This one is absolutely breathtaking. I think we have a winner. How's everything?" She got up to kiss Penny's cheek, then sat again, crossing one long leg over the other. Her red hair was perfectly curled, her green eyes glinted, and she wore a long blue silk shirt with black pants underneath.

"Everything's good. Well, okay, not good." Penny swallowed. She wasn't being entirely truthful, but did it help to bleed all over her friends? She'd never been one to do that. She always put up a veneer of strength and resilience even when she didn't feel it. Although with all her high school girlfriends back together, for the first time in years, she wanted to spill, to tell them everything on her mind.

Bea sat down with them, puffing slightly. "There, I'm done for now. I only have two customers, and they're satisfied. But if anyone else comes in, I'll have to jump up and wait on them. Sorry!"

"That's fine," Evie replied. "Don't mind us—we're happy to chat patiently. Aren't we, Penny?"

"Of course. Very happy."

Bea hurried off to get them each a coffee and a plate of goodies to eat, then sat again.

"Phew. You make me tired just watching you," Penny exclaimed.

"This job is harder than I thought it'd be." Bea wiped sweat from her forehead with the back of her hand.

"But do you like it?" Evie asked. "That's the real question."

"I love it." Bea sighed. "I'm getting used to the physical exertion. I think that over time, I'll be better at it, and then it will all come together beautifully. Right now, I'm constantly reacting to things I didn't realise I had to do — paperwork, licences, timing for ordering supplies, vendor requirements, that kind of thing."

"I know what you mean," Penny said. "I remember that when I started the refuge, it took me a while to figure everything out. I'm still not very good at it."

"What are you talking about?" Evie asked. "You're amazing. I don't know how you manage it all."

Penny held her breath for a moment. Should she say something? If she did, she knew exactly what would happen—her beautiful friends would offer to help. She also knew none of them could afford it. No, she should keep her troubles to herself. Bothering other people with her mistakes wasn't fair to them.

"Oh, nothing," she replied. "Don't mind me."

"How's that delicious nemesis of yours going?" Evie's eyes twinkled with delight.

Penny huffed. "He's not delicious."

"Um..." Bea sipped her coffee.

"Well, maybe he is. But I don't think of him that way. And he's fine. He visited, and we had a really nice talk."

"Well, that is good news." Evie took a bite out of a small purple macaron. "Wow, Bea, you've outdone yourself. This is divine."

Bea's cheeks pinked. "Thank you. So glad you like it. I've been working on perfecting that recipe for years."

"I think you've done it." Evie winked at her friend.

"I had another visitor that same day," Penny continued as

she picked up a small caramel slice. She took a bite and almost forgot her train of thought as the sweetness filled her mouth.

"Oh, yes?" Bea enquired, one eyebrow quirked.

Penny swallowed. "A little girl, Samantha Norton. Do you know her?"

Bea shook her head. Evie's eyes narrowed. "I don't think so, but that name is familiar."

"Isn't Norton Betsy's last name?" Bea asked.

"That's right," Penny agreed. "I asked her if she knew Betsy, but she said no. Anyway, she looks a bit neglected, and I keep seeing her around the place on her own during school hours. It seems like no one is making her go to school or taking care of her while her dad's at work."

"How old is she?" Bea asked, then sipped her coffee.

"She told me she's ten. But she looks younger, I think. Not that I'm an expert on the subject. But she's very thin."

"We should ask Betsy about it. Maybe she'll know more." Evie set down her coffee cup and crossed her arms.

"I really want to do something. I don't think she has a mother in her life."

"I'm going to see if Betsy's around." Bea quickly sent a text message. Her phone dinged almost immediately. "She says she's shopping next door and will be right over."

A few minutes later, after they'd talked about Bea's children and their visit, Betsy appeared at the front door. She hurried to their table, out of breath, her wild grey curls flung in every direction, and sat down with a humph. She wore a brightly coloured tunic and leather sandals, with a thin silk scarf wound loosely around her neck.

"It's hot out there today. Hard to believe it's almost winter, I wish summer would give up already and leave."

Penny laughed. "I know what you mean. We only get two seasons here, and they're almost identical."

They all exchanged pleasantries, and after Bea got a coffee

for Betsy and there was a lapse in conversation, Penny spoke up.

"Betsy, I met a little girl a few days ago called Samantha Norton. She wouldn't be related to you by any chance, would she?"

Betsy's face paled. "You met Sam?"

Penny hesitated. "Uh, yes. Are you okay?"

Betsy leaned back in her chair. "I'm fine. I haven't seen her in a while, that's all."

"She said she didn't know you."

Betsy shrugged. "She wouldn't remember. It was a long time ago."

"But aren't you related?" Bea asked.

"She's my granddaughter."

Penny's eyebrows rose skyward. It was unusual for a grandchild not to recognise the name of her grandmother.

"We're estranged," Betsy continued. "My son doesn't want anything to do with me, so he's kept me away from her."

"Even though you both live on the island?" Evie asked, her eyes wide. "That seems impossible — it's such a small community."

"We make it work. We don't tend to run in the same circles. He stays away from Kellyville for the most part. He works on the mainland, so I rarely see him."

"I'm really sorry to hear that," Penny said. "I can't imagine how hard that must be. My parents moved away, but if they were here, I'd want to spend every moment I could with them. I miss them so much."

Betsy reached out a hand to pat Penny's. "You're a sweet girl and a good daughter. Where did you see Sam?"

"She came to the refuge a few days ago, and I fed her cake. Then I saw her playing on the side of the road today, alone. She should be in school, shouldn't she?"

Betsy sighed. "Yes, she should." She fell quiet and stirred sugar into her coffee.

"Maybe you could talk to your son?" Bea asked.

Betsy's lips pulled tight. "I wish I could. He won't see me."

"Have you tried lately?" Evie's face was lined with compassion.

"Not lately. I suppose I could give it another shot. He can't hold onto the hurt forever, surely."

"I've given Sam my phone number and told her to call me. If she does, I can let you know, and maybe you can see each other," Penny offered.

Betsy met her gaze. "I'd like that. Thank you."

"What happened between the two of you?" Bea asked, her voice gentle.

"It was his wife. I didn't approve of her, and I told him so. He said I couldn't be part of their lives, but then she left him and Sam. I was right, although I get no pleasure out of it. I genuinely wish I hadn't been."

"Of course you do," Bea mused with a shake of her head. "Those things are so difficult to navigate."

"He's always been a bit of a hothead. I struggled with him when he was young, but I loved him. He doesn't seem to recall any of that, apparently."

"Maybe he does now. You should see if he'll give you another chance."

Betsy nodded. "You're right—I will. I can't bear to think that little Sam is being neglected. My son works hard and he's a good father, but she needs her grandmother."

"I think you're right," Penny said. She hated to see the pain in Betsy's eyes, but she was grateful there might be a solution for Sam's situation. And the fact that the solution might well include the care of a loving grandmother was all the more perfect because it was Betsy, one of Penny's favourite people.

She couldn't believe she'd never heard the story before. She vaguely recalled something about Betsy's son from years ago, but she'd assumed he'd moved away and had never really thought about it. It amazed her how much pain and suffering the people around her could hide from everyone they knew.

Fifteen

THE LIBRARY SMELLED of old books and rose potpourri. Bea let her finger trace along the spine of a book, then she walked down the aisle, following the line of books with her fingertips as she read the titles to herself. There were so many books, and this was only one library out of thousands, all over the world. Books on every subject imaginable, as well as every fiction genre and style. It was hard to believe so many people had put pen to paper over the years and written whatever was in their head for others to read. She couldn't imagine doing that.

Give her a cake to bake any day of the week, but she wouldn't bleed herself dry on a page.

Evie, Taya and Penny were seated at a long rectangular table with a microfiche machine at one end. Taya sat in front of the machine, feeding microfiche across the lens and whispering what she found to the others. Bea sat with them and crossed one leg over the other. She leaned forward.

"What is it?"

Taya pushed her chair away from the machine. "Nothing about Penny's grandmother's murder yet. We haven't found the exact date, since Penny isn't sure of it. We only have the year to go by. And there's a lot of news that year, if you can believe it."

Bea huffed. "On Coral Island? How much could've happened in one year?"

"Oh, you'd be surprised," Evie said, nudging an old newspaper across the table towards Bea. "Look at this — there was a pumpkin growing competition, of all things. Then they had a dance, and someone switched off the electricity in the middle of everything, putting them all in the dark. It was a big scandal. Someone's wife kissed someone else's husband, which they all saw as soon as the power came back on."

"Wow, what a disaster," Bea said with a smirk. "The island was salacious back then, apparently. It's nothing like that now. A very upstanding community."

"As far as you know," Penny said with one eyebrow quirked.

"Oh, do tell," Taya said.

Penny drew a fingers across her lips like a zipper. "Never."

The old librarian, Mrs Gossamer, glared at them from her desk at the front of the library. Bea clamped her lips shut and did her best not to giggle. The librarian had been there since she was in primary school, and whenever she saw that tightly pulled grey bun and the half-moon glasses perched on a thin nose, she felt like she was a child getting in trouble for making too much noise all over again.

"Careful. We're going to be expelled from the library," she hissed.

"Does anyone else feel eight years old?" Taya asked.

Bea nodded furiously.

The others stifled a fit of giggles.

"Let's keep investigating," Bea suggested, pulling a pile of newspapers towards her. They were old, and the pages were worn. Some of the printing was smudged or faded. She scanned through headlines, turning the pages as gently as she could manage.

"So, we're looking for any mention of Mary Brown from 1977 or 1978. That's the year Penny thinks she was killed because it happened right after she was born. Am I getting the details correct, Pen?" Bea asked, her finger paused on a story headline.

"That's right," Penny agreed. "Although I could be wrong about the timing and I don't want to call mum about it, since it only upsets her. But let's start there and see what we find."

Before long, Bea's back hurt and her eyes were tired. She found her reading glasses in her purse and slipped them on, then continued her search. Finally, she stumbled across an article from November 15th 1978 with the headline *Grandmother murdered*.

"Look at this!" she said.

Another glare from Mrs Gossamer and she lowered her voice.

"I found it."

The other women gathered around in a semicircle, and she read the article in a hushed tone.

"Mrs Mary Brown was found stabbed to death..."

"Oh, horrible," Evie declared.

"...on the back porch of her house on the beach near Blue Lake at seven p.m. yesterday evening. The murder weapon wasn't found, and no one else was home at the time of the attack. She was discovered by her daughter, Ruby, when she returned from rehearsals for the school play on the evening ferry."

"Your mum was an actress?" Taya asked Penny.

Penny shrugged. "Not really. I think she painted the scenery and was a background extra or something. But she does love to sing."

"So, your mother came home from school late and found

your grandmother dead on the back porch. How old were you then?"

"One year old. I think my grandmother was caring for me at the time," Penny said, her brow furrowed. "Poor Mum. I know she was heartbroken over it. She found me crying in my cot."

"Where was your grandfather?" Taya asked.

"He'd died years earlier."

"It must've been a nightmare for your mother. And you told us your dad wasn't in the picture. Is that right?"

"From what I know, he left before I was born, and Mum was on her own. But she was only sixteen, so perhaps he was very young as well. Of course, she won't say a word about him, which is infuriating. I've given up asking, but I used to be obsessed with finding out anything I could about him. He is my father, after all."

"That's understandable," Bea replied, trying to imagine how she'd feel if she didn't know the identity of one of her parents. It would be a constant itching at the back of her mind, pushing her to learn the truth.

She continued reading. "Look at this. It says there was a possible witness, a Mrs Betsy Norton."

All of the women exchanged a curious glance.

"What are the chances...?" Penny crossed her arms over her chest. "We spoke to her yesterday about her granddaughter, and now we're running across her name in the newspaper as a possible witness to my grandmother's murder."

"That's a very strange coincidence," Taya admitted.

"It's very bizarre, but probably doesn't mean anything. Although I'm surprised she's never mentioned it," Evie added, her nose wrinkling. "Should we talk to her about it?"

"I don't see why not," Bea said.

"But wouldn't she have told us before now if she wanted us to know?" Penny asked.

"You'd think so, but then it did happen a long time ago."

"I've spoken with her a hundred times in my life, and she's never mentioned she knew anything about my grandmother's death," whispered Penny.

"I don't think we should jump to any conclusions until we speak to her," Bea said in her most comforting tone. "Let's wait to hear the facts."

* * *

On her way back to the cottage, Bea stopped by her father's house to see if Harry and Dani were there. They were, the three of them playing a game of Scrabble together on the deck. Beatrice poked her head through the back door and asked if anyone would like a drink, since she was making one for herself, and all three turned her down, as they had glasses dotted around the table already.

Relieved at not having to serve anyone else for at least a few more minutes, she mixed herself a pitcher of sangria and carried that with an empty glass out to the deck, then sat with a grunt.

"That's a big drink you have there." Dad offered her a raised eyebrow.

She sighed. "I've had a big day."

When her glass was full, she gulped a mouthful of sangria, then put her feet up on an empty chair to look out over the cliff to the ocean beyond. The world was right again — the peacefulness of the coastal scene soothed her soul, and the company renewed her strength.

"It's good to be home," she murmured.

"Did you have a good day, Mum?" Dani asked.

"It was busy."

"I'll come in and help again tomorrow morning, if you like."

"That would be great. Thanks."

Harry smiled at her. "Can I do anything to help?"

"Would you like to make dinner? Because I don't think I can stand up for another minute."

"Happy to — I make a fantastic frozen pizza."

"Perfect," she replied.

After she'd rested a while, she got up and went inside to put on some music. A relaxing melody floated through the surround sound speaker system, and she lay on the couch, eyes shut, to let it wash over her. She didn't know or care who the artist was—she loved to enjoy music that slackened her jaw, loosened her tight muscles and helped ease away the tension of the day.

She felt her father's presence before he spoke. He settled into his armchair, and the leather creaked.

"How are you coping with it all?"

"It's fine. I'll get there. I love the space, and the people are wonderful. I can try out recipes and bake, and other people enjoy it, so there's a lot of satisfaction in it. I'm tired—that's all."

"Understandable. I'm coming over tomorrow to do those jobs around the place you asked me to do."

"Thanks, Dad. But not if it's too much for you."

He waved her off. "No trouble at all. I'm not dead yet."

"Don't even joke about that," she warned him, and he laughed.

"It happens to us all."

"I'm painfully aware of that. Speaking of which, do you remember when Penny's grandmother, Mary Brown, was killed?"

His smile faded. "Of course. That was a horrible tragedy. The whole island was shaken by it. Why do you ask?"

"The girls and I are looking into it."

"Why would you do that?"

She sat up, her eyebrows knitting together. His tone was defensive, and his reaction surprised her. "What do you mean?"

"It's old news. Let it go."

"Why does this bother you so much, Dad?"

He shook his head but didn't respond, instead staring out the back window at the children who were flicking ice-cold water at each other and squealing as Harry chased Dani around the deck.

"I found some old photographs in the wall of my cottage when we were renovating."

"I remember that," Dad replied.

"It turns out they were photos of Penny's beach house..."

"Yes?" he said, as though irritated at how slowly she was speaking.

"Photos of her family and of Rowan's family — you know, the Clementses?"

He sighed. "I know the Clementses, and I know the beach house. What's your point?"

"I'm not sure really, only that it got us interested in Penny's history. Her grandmother is in some of the photos, and Penny told us she was killed. So, we were down at the library looking for more information, and we discovered something strange."

"Oh?" He leaned forward.

"It seems the murderer was never caught."

"I knew that." He relaxed into his chair.

"But we also found Betsy Norton's name in the article — apparently, she was one of the witnesses for the case. It doesn't say what she saw, but don't you think it's strange that she never said anything to Penny about it?"

He lurched to his feet, his fists clenched. "Just stop it. Let the past stay in the past."

She stood as well, reaching out to comfort him. "Dad, what's wrong?"

His eyes glistened with unshed tears. "Your mum was obsessed with the case before her death as well. After everything that happened, I would be happy never to talk about it again for as long as I live. I don't want you to follow in her footsteps."

He stormed from the lounge room and out the front door, slamming it behind him. Beatrice stared after him, astonished. Her heart thudded against her rib cage. She understood him connecting it with her own mother's death, but his words only brought more questions to mind than answers. Her mother had been obsessed with Mary Brown's murder ... but why? What did it have to do with her, or with Bea's family? And why was Dad so upset that she wanted to talk about it?

Sixteen

THE MOONLIGHT LIT a silver trail along the beach, and stars twinkled in the partially clouded sky overhead. Penny sat on the second step leading up to her porch door and leaned back to study the sky. It was beautiful. A world full of stars, some bright, some dim, like dot art on a black canvas.

She was still damp from her surf earlier, her wetsuit pulled low about her waist, but her stomach growled with hunger. With a sigh of disappointment at having to tear her gaze away from the heavens, she took an outside shower, then went inside to change and make herself some dinner. Before she got started cooking scrambled eggs and pancakes, her favourite breakfast-for-dinner combination, she hesitated with her phone in hand.

A message had come through with a notification that glared bright in the dim hall light. She stared at it a moment, then shouted for joy. The grant had been approved. The refuge would live another day.

With a flick of her finger, she switched on the kitchen light and set about looking for her frying pan, which she found in the dishwasher, then stopped again to stare at her phone. The message said she should complete the appropriate paperwork to have the money transferred to her account. The attachment was twenty pages long.

Her heart sank. Twenty pages of paperwork? She needed the money yesterday, but with her schedule the way it was, she wouldn't have time to fill out the forms until Thursday night. That was five days away. And she was exhausted after a full week of work, plus gardening around the house and cleaning most of the day — Saturday was designated time for domestic duties.

A thought popped into her head — Rowan had told her she could call him when she needed help. He was good at paperwork. As a journalist, he spent his life writing, filling out forms and working on computers. Perhaps she should make the call. She hated to be needy. Hated needing him for anything. But maybe it was time she made herself a little more vulnerable. She didn't have to be Superwoman and do everything on her own all the time. At least, that's what her mother always told her whenever she wore herself out trying to manage alone.

"Fine," she said to herself. "I'll call him. It's not a big deal. He offered, he's a friend ... sort of . . . and anyway, I need the help. Otherwise, I'll be up all night doing this."

A cat slunk around the corner and into the kitchen. It mewed at her.

"I know, Bart, I'm talking to myself. But I'm not crazy, I promise," she said to the cat, who rubbed himself against her legs, tail raised high.

She dialled and waited, heart pounding. His voice sent a thrill up her spine she wasn't expecting.

"My grant was approved, and I have twenty pages of paperwork..."

"Say no more," he replied. "I'm coming over."

"I'll make dinner," she said.

"Great—I'm starving. I'll bring the wine."

* * *

By the time Rowan arrived at her house, the eggs were ready and served at the table on sourdough toast. The pancakes were slathered in butter and piled high on a plate, and she'd brewed a batch of steaming hot coffee. Although she wasn't sure either of them should imbibe caffeine right now since Rowan was always high energy and she was extremely nervous about him coming over. In fact, she'd almost called him back three times to cancel, but had talked herself out of it.

It made no sense for the two of them to spend time together. They didn't get along, they drove each other crazy, and her brother wouldn't be happy if he heard about it. No matter how much she convinced herself it was none of his business, she still jumped when she heard the car door slam outside and wondered for a moment if it was Rob home from the mainland early before realising it was Rowan.

With a slow intake of breath to calm herself, she hurried to answer the door and let him in with bright, cheery conversation, completely out of character for her usual quiet, subdued self.

He listened with a slight smile on his face for several seconds before putting a hand on her shoulder, looking her in the eye and saying, "You seem a little wound up. Are you okay?"

She blinked. "Fine. I'm fine. Would you like coffee?"

"No, thanks. I don't drink caffeine at this time of night." He sat at the table across from her. "Are you worried about the paperwork? Or is there something else?"

That was when she sat at the table, held Bart as he purred on her lap, and told Rowan about the murder investigation she and her friends were undertaking and how it'd brought up issues she hadn't thought about in years. How she was concerned for a little girl who'd shown up one day at the refuge and wormed her way into Penny's heart. There were so many things on her mind that had her nerves all twisted up.

But the one thing she didn't tell him was that he'd overturned her nice, happy little existence, where everything made sense, and elicited feelings she thought were long behind her.

Finally, she stopped and held her breath, waiting for his response. She'd said too much, revealed too big a piece of herself to him. Regret swamped her.

"You're carrying a lot of things around on your shoulders. I'm not surprised you're anxious. Let's tackle one thing at a time, starting with the paperwork, and go from there." He smiled at her, and her shoulders lowered. His face was open and caring, his posture relaxed. He didn't judge her. Wasn't going to make a smart quip like he usually did. She'd been waiting for the remark that would drive a knife through her heart, but it didn't come.

"Okay, let's do it."

They sat at her computer, side by side, working. As they did, they talked together about the past and the future. His hopes and dreams, her plans and procrastination. They laughed over the mistakes he'd made or the times she'd fallen on her face. And slowly her heart opened, piece by piece, until she'd forgotten all about guarding it from him or that she'd once seen him as the enemy.

When they completed the final section of the form, she submitted the details, and it was done. It hadn't been nearly as cumbersome a process as she'd thought it would be. At least, not with Rowan's help. They'd had fun together, and the time had flown. She couldn't believe it was almost midnight by the time they finally switched off her computer. But just as she pressed the button, the entire house fell into darkness.

"What on earth?" Rowan's disembodied voice floated in the air between them.

"Oh, no," she said.

"Maybe you have a short?"

She sighed. It wasn't a short. "No, I don't think that's it."

"Well, what is it?"

The admission embarrassed her. "I've been holding off on paying my bill. Just until I some money in my account. The refuge is taking everything I have right now, and I thought they'd give me a bit more time."

He grunted. "Apparently not. You should've said something. You can't go without electricity just so your animals are fed."

"They need it more than I do."

"Okay, fair enough. Do you have any candles, or are we going to have to feel our way out of the office? Because I may get a little handsy, and you can't hold me accountable for that." He laughed.

Though he couldn't see it, she rolled her eyes even as a smile drifted across her mouth. "No need to worry. I've got you covered."

"What a shame," he said. She could imagine him winking.

She opened the desk drawer and pulled out a torch. Then the two of them walked to the kitchen, where she lit some candles and spread them around the house. They ended up on the back deck, seated in chairs side by side with a bottle of wine between them as they listened to the ocean. Around them, candles flickered.

"Can I please give you enough money to get your power back on tomorrow?" he asked quietly.

Relying on anyone else wasn't something she was used to doing. She'd been supporting herself since she was eighteen.

129

Her parents had given her the beach house and the land for the refuge, but other than that, she'd had to manage on her own. And she liked it that way. She was beholden to no one and owed nothing. It meant she could be in control. No one could tell her what to do or how to live. But she needed his help. "Thank you. I'll pay you back."

"Of course you will. But there's no rush."

"It's all harder than I thought it would be." She sighed in the darkness, her throat aching.

He reached out and took her hand in his larger one, enveloping it completely. The warmth of his touch made her want to cry. "Everything always is."

"How do people manage it?"

"What—life?"

"Life, business, running a charity."

He looked at her. "You know most people don't try to run a wildlife refuge on their own, right? It's virtually impossible, yet you've managed to do it for years. Somehow you've kept the lights on—" he waved a hand around "—until tonight. That's actually pretty amazing. I hope you know that."

She swallowed. "Do you think so?"

"Of course. It's incredible. *You're* incredible."

"Thanks." She sniffled as tears threatened.

He squeezed her hand but didn't let go. She wanted him to pull her close, kiss her tears away, tell her everything was going to be okay. But if he did, what would she do then? She wasn't ready for that level of intimacy. She'd always pushed him away in the past. Would she do it again? She couldn't trust herself not to. And how would Rob would feel about it?

"You know, this is actually pretty romantic," he said, grinning at her in the golden swathe of candlelight. "I couldn't have planned it better if I tried."

Perhaps she should forget about the past and focus on the present. After all, she'd clearly misjudged him for all those years. He wasn't the person she'd thought he was, or maybe he'd changed. Either way, she was starting to feel things for him she'd been running from her whole life. Nerves twirled and fluttered in her stomach like butterflies at the thought of where this could lead if she let go of control.

Seventeen

THE WATER WAS clear and the reef was a plethora of colours under the dazzling sunlight that glinted as the waves surged back and forth across it. It was a small reef off the beach beside the headland where her father's house perched high above them, its peaked roof like a shadow behind the piles of black rocks that scalloped the cliffs.

Beatrice, Dani, Harry and Bradford snorkelled around the rocks and over the reef together while Dad watched from the shore, seated in a folding chair that Bradford had insisted on bringing down the narrow path for him.

Parrotfish followed Beatrice's flippers as she kicked. She looked back over her shoulder at them as she glided through the water. There were a variety of types of fish hovering above the reef. A clown fish ducked into an anemone as she sailed overhead. A small red coral trout peeped from behind a piece of coral and then ducked back behind it again when it spotted Bea.

She emerged through the surface of the water and spat out her mouthpiece before spitting out salt water with a cough. She pushed her mask up over her forehead and looked around, swimming in place. The others had made their way towards the shore, and Dad was folding up his chair. The sun was high overhead. It was time to go back to the house. The children were headed to Sydney on the noon ferry, and she'd dreaded the farewell for days.

It'd been so nice to have them stay with her on the island. She wished they could stay forever, although she knew it was good for them to build a life for themselves, and university was a big part of that. But she couldn't help being selfish — she missed them. And now that Aidan had his new daughter and she rarely saw him, she was lonelier than she'd been willing to admit. She still had her friends, and her father and brother of course, but she missed Aidan and her kids.

She knew she could manage on her own, and she was doing rather well at that. But having them with her for two weeks reminded her how much she enjoyed their company. They'd become lovely, kind and thoughtful adults, and she couldn't be prouder of them.

She put her mask and snorkel back in place and kicked towards the shore. On the beach, the sun baked her back within moments, and she was suddenly very glad that she'd worn a wetsuit. She'd had enough of sunburn to last her a lifetime.

"Ready to go up?" she asked.

Dani nodded.

Harry smiled. "You going to miss us, Mum?"

Bea laced an arm around his waist. "More than you can possibly know. But I'm glad you're happy in your dorm and with your friends. Please call me if you need anything. I can be in Sydney in no time at all."

"It's a long way."

"I don't mind. I'll be there in a flash if you need me."

They walked slowly up the path together, talking over the semester ahead and what each of the children would study, what they'd need and how they felt about it all. By the time they'd showered, packed and eaten a light meal, Bea was ready to drive them to the ferry and had pushed her emotions down so she could tell them goodbye without crying.

She waved as the ferry left the shore, then sighed as the boat accelerated across the bay. When she could no longer see them, she climbed back into her car and sobbed for a few moments against the steering wheel. She pulled herself together and drove home to the cottage.

There were a few hours for her to rest before she had another task to complete — she'd promised Aidan she would come to his house to help him through a visit from Grace's mum, Kelly. And tonight, Kelly was having dinner with them all at Aidan's. Bea had agreed to cook and to host so Aidan could spend his nervous energy managing the conflict he'd already predicted might erupt between the mother and daughter.

With her feet up and a book in her hands, she sipped a cup of coffee in her living room, enjoying the quiet of the cottage, the whisper of the ocean, the twitter of birds weaving through the trees around the structure. A light breeze floated through the open windows. Bea relished those moments to relax her tired body and her overstimulated mind. As much as she loved having visitors, there was a certain satisfaction in having the cottage all to herself once again.

She'd only made it through a few pages before the phone rang. With a groan, she stared at it on the table next to her chair. Maybe she could simply ignore it. But what if it was one of the kids with a problem catching their flight? She turned the phone over and saw Aidan's name on the screen.

"Hello?"

"Bea, I don't know what to do. Can you please help me find Grace?"

She sat up straight. "What do you mean? Where is she?"

"I don't know." His voice was panicked. "We had an argument about the dinner tonight. She said she hates her mother and never wants to see her again. I tried to smooth things over, told her she shouldn't say 'hate,' that she should give her mum a chance. After all, she's raised her..."

"And she didn't take that well, I'm guessing." Bea rubbed a hand over her face.

"No, she didn't. She stormed out of here, slammed the door and took off in my car. I don't know where she's gone, and I don't have a vehicle to follow her in and she doesn't have a license. If Kelly gets here this afternoon and I tell her I can't find our daughter..."

"It could go badly," Bea finished.

"And I'm worried about her. She was really angry."

"I'm sure she's fine. She just needs a little break to cool off." Bea had a sudden thought flit through her mind. "I have an idea about where she might be. I'll go looking for her. You just relax and prepare for this evening. I'll let you know how I go."

"Thank you, thank you... I really appreciate it. I don't know what to do here. I'm going crazy."

"Welcome to parenting a teen." She sighed. "There's only so many places she could go on the island. Try not to get too upset. Teens can have big emotions, but they usually come around once you explain things to them in a loving and sensible way."

"I hope you're right."

She hung up the phone and stood to her feet with a grunt. So much for her alone time with a good book. She gulped down a mouthful of coffee as she carried the cup to the kitchen, then rinsed it out. It didn't take long to pack the car with the things she'd need to make dinner that evening, along with a change of clothes and some makeup. Then she drove to

Betsy's fishing hole, hoping the whole way there that she was right about Grace's movements.

When she pulled up alongside the road, she saw Aidan's truck parked a little farther down.

She texted Aidan. *I found her. Will bring home as soon as I can.* The phone only had one bar, and as soon as she stepped out of the car and began the climb down the winding track to the hidden cove, that bar disappeared. If Aidan responded, she wouldn't know until she was driving again.

Grace was seated in exactly the same place, behind the large black rock, that she had been the last time Bea saw her there. She had her legs bent up, her arms hugging them, and her chin rested on her knees as she stared into the water lapping at her toes.

"Hi, Grace," Bea said.

Grace glanced up at her, startled. Her eyebrows knit together when she saw who it was. "What do you want?"

"I came here looking for you. Aidan's worried about you."

She crossed her legs and glared. "I'm fine."

"I can see that. Do you mind if I join you?"

Grace shrugged.

Bea climbed over the rocks and sat on the sand beside her. She didn't speak for a few minutes, and the two of them sat side by side, listening to the sounds of the ocean and the birds. It was the perfect hiding place. No one would find them there. No wonder Betsy had adopted it as her own getaway for so long.

"Are you nervous about your mother visiting?"

"No. Why would I be nervous?"

"I don't know. Maybe you're worried that she won't like Aidan or that they'll argue."

"She wants me to go home with her."

"And you don't want to?"

Another shrug.

"I'm sure she misses you."

Grace sighed. "I know. But we fight so much, I hate it there. She told me I had to leave if I didn't change my behaviour. I'm only fifteen. I can't believe she'd do that to me." Tears filled her eyes, and her voice broke over the words.

Bea ached at the girl's pain. Rejection like that was a hard thing to face. "Do you think she meant it, or was she speaking in anger?"

"I don't know. I wasn't waiting around to find out. I can't believe she'd kick out her own daughter just because we argued."

"It probably made you feel like her love was conditional."

Grace nodded and wiped her nose with the back of her hand. "She only wants me when I'm good."

"It's difficult getting older and having to deal with these kinds of conflicts, but learning to face them now will really help you in life. If you can handle it in a mature way — really listen to what your mother is saying, try not to explode at her but instead, talk it through — you'll be able to cope with anything that comes your way in life."

Grace looked at her, making eye contact for the first time. "Do you think so?"

"Definitely. This is the hard stuff. Other things are easy in comparison. The people we love most can hurt us more than anyone else. But that means we also have to forgive them more often. Because relationships are tough — we have to fight for them or we won't make it."

"Do you and your daughter fight?"

Bea's eyes widened. "Oh, yeah, definitely. Especially when she was your age. We fought a lot. Over all kinds of things. But we made sure to talk things through and to forgive because our connection was important to both of us. And now we have an amazing relationship."

"You still loved her, even after the fights?" Grace's tear-soaked eyes tugged at Bea's heart.

"Of course. A mother never stops loving her kids, no matter what. I don't know your mother, but if you feel unsafe around her, I'm sure Aidan will let you stay here."

"No, I don't feel unsafe." Grace wiped her tears from her cheeks with a thumb.

"Maybe hear her out tonight, and you can decide what you want to do after that."

"You don't think Aidan will make me go with her?"

Bea shook her head. "No, I don't think he will. He cares about you and wants what's best for you."

"But what if I don't see him again?"

"I really don't believe he'd let that happen. You're stuck with him now." Bea smiled. "He's a very loyal and caring person."

Grace stared at the ocean again. The two of them watched a seagull pluck a small fish from the water's surface and fly off with it to perch on top of the cliffs.

The girl sighed. "I suppose I have to face her."

"I think you should. If you don't try to make amends now, this rift between you could get worse. And I know you don't want that."

Grace nodded, then went back to staring over the water in silence. Bea leaned her back against a rock to wait. When Grace was ready, they'd drive home. She only hoped the dinner went well that evening, for Aiden's sake as well as Grace's.

Eighteen

THE DRIVE back to Aidan's was a brief one. Since Grace didn't have a driver's licence, Bea drove carefully behind her to make sure she was okay. She'd clearly been taught the basics and knew how to navigate the road, although no doubt Aidan would have a serious conversation with her about boundaries and respect for himself and for the law.

Aiden's house at Prospect Point appeared more homely than the last time Bea had visited. The garden of spiky dry-weather plants was better established, and when they walked inside, she saw he'd bought some warmer pieces of decor to make the place more welcoming such as a wall of family photographs, cushions, throw rugs and an upright piano.

The walls were white, and the house was made up of various levels with high, sloping ceilings accented by natural timber beams and far too many windows for Bea's liking. It was almost like walking through a fish tank. Long, plush curtains hung beside each window so he could at least gain some privacy at night. But the place suited Aidan — modern, sleek, impressive while her cottage seemed to reflect herself — small, squat and homely. She smiled at her own observation —

the two of them were so different. Perhaps that was one of the reasons it hadn't worked out between them.

Aidan was relieved to see Grace, but didn't make a big deal out of it to her face. He hugged her warmly then asked her if she was okay.

"I'm fine," she said.

"I'm sorry we fought," he replied, "and later we'll have to talk about what you did..."

"I know. I'm sorry too. I'm going to get changed." Grace jogged up the stairs to her room.

Aidan faced Bea with arched eyebrows. "I have no idea how you found her so quickly, but thank you."

"It's our little secret," Bea said, mimicking locking her mouth and tossing aside the key.

He laughed. "Thank goodness. I was really worried."

"She's anxious, that's all. When teens get anxious, they don't always recognise that's what's going on and they often don't have the tools to manage it."

"Kelly will be here in an hour. I've put together an appetiser platter, and the drinks are chilling."

"Perfect," Bea said. "I'll take my things to the kitchen and get started on dinner."

"Did I tell you how much I appreciate this?"

"Only a dozen times," she replied.

"Then I'll say it again. Thank you. I've been so busy with the development I'm working on and taking care of Grace, I haven't had a moment to think about tonight. I know you're busy as well, but you're such a great cook..."

"I'm happy to do it. There's nothing I like more than to cook good food for people. And I'm pretty fond of you as well." She grinned. "I want tonight to go well. I don't know what Kelly is like, or what she's coming here to do, but I hope she and Grace find reconciliation and that you're not caught in the middle of anything."

He sighed. "I have to confess, I have no idea what to expect either."

"Whatever it is, I'm here for you, and you'll get through it."

He raised a hand to cup her cheek. His touch warmed her. His hand was gone again as quickly, his cheeks pink. "I'm going to take a shower."

She bustled outside, letting the door fall shut quietly behind her. She leaned against the frame and let her eyes drift shut. It hurt to be so close to him, to share these moments of life with him when she couldn't touch him, when he couldn't hold her close. It'd been the most natural thing in the world that they were together, and now that they'd been pulled apart, it hurt more than she'd ever thought possible after such a short reunion.

The truth was, it'd brought to the surface all the feelings she'd repressed years ago when Aidan ended things. Only this time, she knew he hadn't rejected her—he was doing his best to cope with a stressful and unexpected situation. Just like his daughter, he needed time to cool down.

With a measured intake of breath, she walked to the car to get her things. Then she hurried back to the kitchen to get started.

* * *

When Kelly arrived at Aidan's house, Bea was in the kitchen putting the finishing touches on her mushroom and truffle pasta with garlic bread and a tossed garden salad. The meal was simple but delicious, and she hoped it would be well received by the others.

She heard Aidan answer the door and took off her apron to go out to meet Grace's mother. She looked a little uncomfortable, but Aidan was charming and welcoming, and she visibly relaxed after he introduced Beatrice. They all chatted for a while together out on the deck.

Kelly was tall and glamorous, with long, thick brown hair that hung halfway down her back. She had hazel eyes bordered by dark lashes. Her figure was curvaceous and her lips impossibly full. She didn't have lines around her eyes like Bea did. How old was she? Clearly old enough for a fifteen-year-old daughter. She was polite but standoffish, and didn't smile when introduced to Beatrice.

Grace came out to join them and caught Bea's eye with a half smile before embracing her mother. Grace was polite if somewhat taciturn, but it was obvious to Bea that Kelly loved her daughter and missed her terribly.

They sat down together to eat. Bea and Aidan both served the meal, then sat opposite one another at his long timber dining table.

"This looks delicious," Kelly said.

"Thank you. I hope it is." Bea adjusted the napkin on her lap.

They all began to eat. Bea was glad to note that the pasta was still warm and the salad was crisp and fresh. Within minutes, Grace excused herself to go to the bathroom. Kelly watched her leave.

"I wanted to thank you, Aidan," Kelly said. "You took in Grace without questions or concerns and treated her with love. I appreciate that. I didn't know where she'd gone, and I was beside myself with worry."

"I was happy to do it," Aidan said. "But as we discussed on the phone, I've been upset about the timing. I wish you'd told me about her right away. I could've been there for her first step, her first word. I could've walked her to school on the first day." His voice broke. "I don't understand why you kept her from me all this time."

She sighed and dabbed her lips with her napkin. "We were

together while you and your wife were separated. When you came to tell me you were reconciling, I didn't know I was pregnant. But I found out soon after. By that time, you'd changed your phone number and moved. You were back with your wife. You both seemed happy, and I didn't want to rock the boat."

"But I told my wife about the relationship. It wasn't a secret." Aidan steepled his hands above his plate.

"I didn't know that. We weren't talking."

"You could've told me," he repeated.

"I should've. I know that now. I'm sorry."

A sound behind Aidan made him turn. Grace stood there, her face sullen. She moved forward and took her seat silently.

Grace picked up her fork.

Aidan faced her. "None of this is your fault, Grace. I don't want you to think I'm upset with you—I'm not. I'm grateful that you came to see me and that I get to know you from now on. I just wish I'd been able to spend more time with you."

"Me too," Grace whispered. "I always wanted a dad, but Mum told me I didn't have one."

Aidan's nostrils flared. Bea could tell he was doing his best to keep from getting angry at Kelly, but she didn't blame him for feeling the way he did. If someone had kept her from seeing her children, she would've been furious as well.

Kelly's face tightened, and she stood to her feet. "I'm not going to sit here and be accused by both of you. I did the best I could. I raised Grace on my own, with no help from anyone. I don't deserve this." She threw her napkin down on the table and marched out the front door, slamming it shut behind her. The sound echoed throughout the spacious house.

Grace stared at her plate. At first Bea resisted the urge to intervene, but one look at Aidan's face told her he was uncertain of what to say.

"Your mum came a long way to see you. We can't change

145

the past—we can only build the future that we want," Bea said gently.

Grace nodded, stood to her feet and hurried to the front door. She stepped outside, and they heard her call after her mother.

"Thank you," Aidan said, running fingers through his hair. "I knew it would be hard, but this is impossible. I can't move past the grief I feel every time I think about the lonely years I've spent wishing I had a family after my wife died, and all that time, Grace was alive, hundreds of kilometres away, wishing she had a father." He shook his head, his eyes flashing. "It makes no sense. It's so unfair."

"You're right—it *is* unfair. But you can't do anything about it now."

"I know that." He groaned. "It's so frustrating."

"Give it time. You'll find a way through this together. This is what having a family is like — it's wonderful, infuriating, impossible, beautiful, overwhelming and a thousand other things. But always worth it."

He laughed hollowly. "My wife and I always had conflict, especially in the early years, but it wasn't like this. This passionate, soul-crushing roller coaster ride."

"Being a parent is different."

"That's true. Should I go after them?"

"I think they can manage this part. Let's eat before it gets cold. Hopefully they'll join us again soon."

They sat and ate, talked about fishing, the weather, snorkelling, her kids on their way back to Sydney and how she felt about it. Ten minutes later, Grace and her mother came back inside and sat at the table. Kelly had red blotches on her neck. Grace's eyes were tear-soaked. But both of them smiled.

"How did you know I like mushrooms so much, Bea?" Grace asked as she piled pasta onto her fork.

"I didn't, but glad to hear it." Bea smiled, twisting her fork into the pasta.

The conversation flowed smoothly and involved plenty of laughter after that. It was as if the initial tension had been broken, the words harboured in heavy hearts for too long had been set free and they were all released to be themselves.

After dinner, Grace packed up the things in the room Aidan had given her, embraced him goodbye and left with Kelly. Aidan promised to come and visit. She said she'd spend part of her school holidays on the island. And while Bea cleaned up in the kitchen, Aidan watched them pull out of the driveway and leave. He lingered outside for a while, and when he came into the kitchen to help Bea, his face was pale and his eyes were glassy.

"Tired?" she asked him.

He nodded. "Exhausted. It's been a long week."

"I'll finish cleaning up, and then you can have the house to yourself. Maybe you should go to bed early, get some rest."

He sighed. "Thank you again. Having you here made all the difference. We may not have been able to resolve things without you. I don't know if Grace would've even been here if you hadn't found her and brought her back."

"You're very welcome. I'm glad I could help. And I think you underestimate yourself and your daughter. You both would've been perfectly fine."

Nineteen

IT WAS a Thursday when Samantha Norton showed up at the wildlife refuge the next time. Penny was busy hosing out one of the bird enclosures when she heard a little voice calling through the fence.

She went to let her in, and this time, the girl didn't hold back. There was no shyness remaining. She chattered nonstop while Penny finished hosing out the enclosure, and she even helped to put everything back in its place afterwards.

"Would you like some cake?" Penny asked. She was better prepared than the last time Sam was there, and had sandwich supplies on hand as well.

Sam nodded vigorously in response, and the two of them went inside to wash up and eat. Sam told her all about school and the issues she was having in her friendship group while Penny made them each a ham sandwich, a glass of milk and a slice of cake. She added a spoonful of Milo to Sam's milk, and they sat side by side at the small kitchen table to eat.

Penny had to admit she was grateful to hear about Sam's friendship problems at the school. Otherwise, she wouldn't be certain the girl attended at all. Her hair remained tangled, her clothes stained and her face ruddy and dirty. But she was happy and chirped like a bird throughout their meal around mouthfuls of sandwich.

Penny excused herself for a moment to message Betsy that Sam was there, and Betsy replied that she was on her way over to see them. So Penny did what she could to occupy the girl until Betsy's arrival. Had she done the right thing? She had no idea. Surely it couldn't be wrong to give a grandmother a chance to know her own grandchild. But what if Sam's father didn't want her to see Betsy? What if there was something else going on that Penny didn't know about?

Anxiety squirmed in her gut while they waited until Sam finally asked her if something was wrong. She pushed a smile onto her face. "No, nothing's wrong. Let's go and see if those wombats are still asleep."

They were watching the wombats snoozing when Betsy buzzed at the gate. Penny let her in and walked with her to where Sam was patting a pademelon with a bandage around its tail.

"What's wrong with this one?" she asked as Betsy stopped beside her. Sam looked up at Betsy without recognition. "Hi."

Betsy squatted beside the girl, her eyes glistening with tears. "Hi, Sam. My name's Betsy. But you can call me Gran."

"Gran?" The girl's eyes widened. "Are you my grandmother?"

Betsy nodded. "Have you heard about me?"

Sam studied her curiously. "I thought you'd be older."

"Oh? I'm pretty old."

Sam's nose wrinkled. "Dad said we couldn't see you anymore."

"I hope he'll change his mind. I've wanted to be with you every single moment since you were born."

"Dad lied?"

"That's not how I'd put it. I think maybe we got our wires crossed. Do you ever get your wires crossed?"

Sam shook her head, brows drawn together. "Uh-uh."

"Grownups sometimes do. It just means we get confused and don't understand something."

"Oh, I get confused a lot."

"So you know what I mean, then?"

Sam nodded. "Do you want to meet this pademelon? Penny lets me feed them."

"I'd love to."

Penny told them she was going to find some food for the kangaroos and pademelons and they could feed all of them at the same time. As she walked away, her nerves faded. The reconciliation gone better than she'd expected. Sam didn't seem bothered by meeting Betsy, and clearly the older woman was delighted.

When she returned, there was someone else waiting at the front gate. She opened it and a middle-aged man barrelled past her and into the enclosure. Penny called after him, asking him to stop, he was on private property, but he ignored her. He found Betsy and Sam by the pademelons almost immediately and hurried to grab Sam by the hand.

"Come on, sweetheart, we have to go. I found your note about coming here, but we can't stay."

"Aww, Dad, I'm feeding the animals. Penny says I have a natural affinity."

"I'm sure you do. But we can't stay." He hesitated, glaring at Betsy. She stepped back, both hands clenched at her sides.

"Let her stay a little longer," Betsy begged in a soft voice.

The man sighed. "You know better, Mum."

"I'm sorry. I had to see her. She's so big now."

"We can talk about it later—not in front of Sam."

"Okay, if that's what you want, Tyler. But won't you let me spend a few more minutes with her? You can't keep her away from her own family forever. And she needs me, I can sense it."

He released Sam's hand. "Okay, fine. I suppose we can spend a few minutes, but then I have to get back to work. I've missed too much as it is."

"Thank you," Betsy said.

Sam grinned. "Can we feed the kangaroos now?"

Penny led them over to where the kangaroos lay about dozing in the sun. A few came closer to be fed, resting on their tails. Penny wasn't sure what to say or do, so she mostly kept quiet and out of the way. Betsy and Tyler continued to talk, and gradually the tension faded. They talked about work, life and the weather. Nothing too deep or personal, but it was progress. And before long, all of them were laughing over some simple knock-knock jokes Sam told.

Finally, it was time for the three of them to leave. Penny walked them to the gate and overheard Tyler agreeing to allow Sam to go to the florist shop after school the following day to spend time with Betsy.

"We haven't fixed things," he said, with a guarded expression. "But I need the help. We can talk more about our issues later. I'm struggling..."

"I'll help you, no strings attached," Betsy promised.

Penny waved goodbye to the trio, who walked away together, Sam in the middle holding hands with her father and grandmother on either side of her.

She was both relieved and happy. The reconciliation could've gone badly for them and for Penny. It wasn't certain she'd done the right thing by letting Sam into the sanctuary or by calling Betsy to come and meet her. Tyler might've been angry. He could've taken his feelings out on Penny. But instead, the encounter seemed to have given him permission to let go of his grudge and try to reconnect with his mother. If they could only forgive whatever had happened in the past and move forward, it would be life-changing for all of them. And perhaps now Sam would have someone to help take care of her so she wouldn't be alone every afternoon.

Once they were gone, Penny locked the front gate, then hurried inside. Rowan had loaned her a small amount of money to tide her over until the government grant came through, and it was time to pay her electricity bill and get the power back on at the beach house. She'd had enough of candlelight and antipasto platters for dinner, although it *had* been extremely romantic. Her cat, Bart, had taken to spending all his time outside on the porch in protest.

She couldn't remember a more romantic evening in her entire life. The memory of it sent a thrill through her. It was hard to believe it'd been with Rowan Clements, though. What was happening between them? Where was this headed? Could it go anywhere? He lived in the USA most of the time—he was a travelling reporter. She was firmly entrenched in island life and her refuge. If there was any chance of a future between them, one of them would have to make an adjustment. He'd already told her he wanted that change, that he was sick of the nomadic life he'd lived for so long. Would he follow through?

Twenty

THE CAFÉ WAS BUSIER than usual. There were customers seated at every table and several waiting in the sitting area in the front corner where Bea had set up some comfortable chairs and pillows. Some wandered around the bookshop browsing while they waited for a table. It was the weekend, and a ferry full of tourists had just arrived on the island.

Beatrice rushed between tables, taking orders and clearing plates and cups. Her two casual workers did the same and were run off their feet. She'd hired someone to cook in the kitchen as well and offered a lunch menu that she thought was delicious, and so far, the customers seemed to agree. Her favourite menu item was from the All-Day Breakfast selection — red velvet sprouted-wheat pancakes with whipped cream cheese and fresh berries drizzled with syrup.

"Can I have a table, please?" a deep voice asked.

She spun around to tell the speaker that the wait was about fifteen minutes and found herself face-to-face with her ex-husband. Preston was fit and tanned. He smiled at her, his teeth impossibly white. He wore a blue coat over a white shirt, unbuttoned at the neck, and a pair of chinos.

"Preston, wow. What are you doing here? The kids are back in Sydney..."

"I know they are. But we have to talk," he said. "Can you sit a while if I get a table and order something?"

"Not for hours, I'm afraid. A big boatload of tourists arrived an hour or so ago, and they're all very hungry."

"I know. I'm one of them," he said. "That's fine—we'll order and wait. We have plenty of time. We're staying overnight."

"We?" Her heart skipped a beat. Had he really brought his fiancée to Coral Island to rub her nose in his perfect new life?

His eyebrows drew upwards. "Yes, I brought Annie with me."

Annie?

Her friend from Sydney? Beatrice was harried. Customers had hands raised all over the café. They needed someone to serve them. She was distracted, but Preston's words rang in her ears.

Why would her friend Annie come to Coral Island without letting her know ahead of time? And wouldn't she be busy with... Come to think of it, she couldn't recall what Annie might be busy with now that her children had left home. But no doubt there was something on her plate. She'd always been far too occupied with her life to visit before now. Perhaps she'd finally succumbed to Bea's invitations and meant to surprise her. But why had Preston said he brought her?

Bea's eyes widened as Annie stepped forward through the throng of customers, a shy smile on her face. Her previously grey bob had been coloured a stylish blonde with honey highlights. Her blue eyes lit up at the sight of Beatrice in her café apron and black uniform, her hair greasy, tucked behind her ears.

"Beatrice, it's been far too long," Annie said, stepping forward to hug Bea.

Bea's mind raced in circles. She couldn't figure out what was happening. Her heart thudded, and her forehead broke out in a sweat. There was a piece to the puzzle that she was missing.

"It's good to see you, Annie." She took a step back, fidgeting with her apron strap. "So, I suppose I should try to find the two of you somewhere to sit."

"No rush," Preston said.

"Here, take a number and we'll buzz you when your table is available." She felt like an air hostess giving instructions to a couple of strangers. Her voice was stilted, her body tense.

"Thanks," Annie replied, taking the buzzer. "We'll be in the delightful little bookshop next door."

The two of them walked past Beatrice, their heads bowed together in conversation. Annie threw her hair back with a flick of the wrist as she laughed at something Preston said. Beatrice watched them go, her brow furrowed.

"Who was that?" Evie asked, coming up suddenly beside her.

"That was my ex-husband, Preston."

"I thought I recognised him. But he looks different somehow."

"He looks happy and well-rested." Beatrice's eyes narrowed. "I barely recognise him myself."

"And is that the famous fiancée?"

"No, it most definitely is not. She's one of my friends from Sydney."

Evie's face registered shock. "Wow … okay. Well, keep me updated. I have to know how this one turns out."

"I can hardly wait to find out for myself." Beatrice's voice dripped with sarcasm.

* * *

The rest of the afternoon, Beatrice worked with a ball of dread in her gut. It wasn't obvious to her what was going on, but several theories rolled around in her head as she cleared plates and farewelled the tourists who were catching the ferry back to the mainland.

Preston and Annie stayed. They'd taken a game of chess from a shelf at the back of the café and were laughing and chattering over their game. Preston was winning, of course. He hated to lose at anything and was always a bad sport when he did. They'd eaten a piece of cake each and drunk two cappuccinos apiece. The sun was dropping slowly over the water, setting it on fire. And Beatrice had a headache that'd begun a half hour earlier at the base of her skull playing bongos on her brain.

When finally the last of her customers left and she'd cleaned up and closed the café, she turned with a sigh to join Preston and Annie at their table. She sat across from Preston.

"I hope you enjoyed your cake and coffee."

"We had a lovely afternoon. Very relaxing," Preston said.

"And the cake was delicious," Annie added.

"I'm so glad you liked it." She hesitated, hoping they'd continue without her peppering them with questions like, What are you doing here? Why did you come all the way to Coral Island when the kids aren't here? What are the two of you doing together? Questions she didn't want to ask, but had to know the answer to.

Preston glanced at Annie, then reached for her hand and took it in his.

Beatrice inhaled a sharp breath at the sight of them with hands linked.

"As you may have guessed, Annie and I are seeing each other," Preston said.

Annie smiled at him, then turned her beam on Beatrice. "We're friends, so I told Preston we had to come and see you in person, to let you know. I hope you can be happy for us."

Beatrice pressed her lips together and gave a quick nod. "I see."

Preston swallowed. "It didn't work out with Geri, and I realise now she was too young for me."

Preston continued. "She stayed in Melbourne, and to be honest with you, I really missed Sydney. So when we broke up, I came back to the city and found a small place in our old neighbourhood."

"Our neighbourhood?" Bea's nostrils flared. This was getting worse and worse by the moment.

"Yes, well, it held so many good memories for me. You weren't there any longer, of course, or the kids. But still, I wanted to be around people I knew, who cared about me. I missed you and the kids more than I was ready to admit. And then I ran into Annie taking a walk one day. We got to talking, and . . . well..."

"The next thing we knew, hours had passed, and we'd hardly noticed." Annie gazed lovingly at Preston as she stroked the back of his hand.

Bea's stomach lurched. "Wow."

"I know. It's so unexpected. We've never connected this way before, but we understood each other like no one ever has before. No offence," Annie continued.

"None taken," Bea replied. "How long has this been going on?"

"About four weeks," Preston replied. "But we're serious about this, Bea. And I need you to sign those divorce papers."

Bea's brows pulled low. "What do you mean? We're already divorced. I signed the papers months ago."

"You missed one of the signatures. Didn't you get the email from my solicitor? We thought everything was done, but there was one line left blank. He said he tried to contact you several times. He has a Melbourne phone number, he told me he's called repeatedly."

Bea slapped a hand to her forehead. "Oh, I did get a call from a Melbourne number a few times, but I thought it was a telemarketer and blocked it. There were no messages..."

"No emails?"

"Not that I saw."

"Well, regardless, things are getting serious between me and Annie, and we'd like to have the divorce finally taken care of, if you don't mind."

What if she did mind? That was a question she'd love to ask while she watched the expression on their lovelorn faces. She wanted to throw her glass of water in those very same faces, but she resisted the urge. How could Annie do this to her? She didn't want Preston back—he was welcome to move on with anyone he wanted. But her friend? Why did it have to be Annie? Out of all her friends from her life in Sydney, Annie had been the kindest, the one she was most likely to stay in touch with. They'd exchanged emails and phone calls several times since Bea moved to the island. And yet Annie hadn't said a word about having issues in her own marriage, let alone dating Bea's ex-husband. Or apparently, her current husband since, according to him, they were still married.

She stood to her feet. "It seems I have some emails to check. And I'm exhausted after working all day. So..."

"We'll get out of your hair," Preston said. "We're staying at the Blue Shoal Inn on the other side of the island. It's supposed to be delightful."

"That's great," Bea said, her voice empty. Maybe he could

try hitting on Taya, another of her friends, while he was there. It was difficult to keep abreast of his dating life, so perhaps he already had. She tried to pull herself together. She couldn't do anything to change Preston, and she'd long ago given up trying. He was an adult; he could do as he wished. And she had no desire to be involved in his life other than as co-parents to their two grown children.

"We're heading back to the mainland tomorrow after we've been on a snorkelling tour. But you can reach me on my mobile number if you need anything before we go. Let me know if you can't find that email, and I'll get my solicitor to resend it."

"Thanks, Preston." She walked them to the door, opened it and stood on the threshold.

"Do you mind if I use your restroom quickly before I go? Two coffees..." Annie patted her stomach apologetically.

"Of course. It's back there," Bea said, pointing toward the end of the café.

Preston watched Annie walk away. "Thanks for being so great about all of this. You've been a real rock for me and the kids for so long, I shouldn't be surprised. But I am."

She chose her words carefully. "I want you to be happy, Pres."

His eyes crinkled at the edges. "You're so wonderful. I hope you find someone who makes you as happy as Annie makes me."

"Thanks." She grunted as he flung his arms around her in a gigantic hug that knocked the breath out of her.

He held her tight, her head pressed to his chest. His heart hammered against his ribs. "I miss this," he whispered.

She wanted to pull free, but his grasp was too strong. "Uh, okay, Pres..."

As she stood there, Aidan's truck pulled up in front of the café and parked. Aidan climbed out. He saw her in Preston's arms, and his eyes widened. Then he shook his head, spun on his heel and launched himself back into the truck. When he accelerated away, the tyres squealed on the asphalt.

"No, wait!" Bea shouted, but her voice was muffled by Preston's shirt.

She wriggled free of his grasp, stepped out onto the street, then sighed in frustration as Aidan's truck disappeared down the road.

"What's wrong?" Preston asked, his brow furrowed.

"Nothing. Everything's fine. It was good to see you, Pres. I hope you enjoy the inn. It's lovely there."

Annie joined them and hugged Bea goodbye. Bea did her best to mimic a tree trunk while Annie wrapped her arms around her awkwardly. "Thanks again, Bea. Good to see you."

Then Annie slipped her hand into Preston's and the two of them walked away, joined hands swinging in time to their footsteps. While Bea watched them go, she wondered why Aidan had come to see her. Did he need something from her? And why was he so ready to leave when he saw her with Preston? They were friends, nothing more. He'd made that perfectly clear. She texted him quickly, but he didn't respond. Then she went inside to finish packing up the cafe for the day, her thoughts in a jumble.

Twenty-One

IT WAS a quiet day at the Blue Shoal Inn. Bea sat in the corner at the large table on her own, staring out the window and sipping a glass of chardonnay. The dining room was decorated in classic style with individually selected retro-style pieces of furniture, a Turkish rug on the floor, a grandfather clock in the corner and a large empty fireplace on one side of the room. The other side was flanked with windows that looked out over the ocean.

Bea was early for their lunch. Taya had some customers to take care of and the others hadn't arrived yet, which was fine with her as it gave her some time to think.

She still hadn't fully processed her feelings about Preston and Annie's surprise visit to the island three days earlier. They'd returned to Airlie Beach to finish their getaway at a luxury resort and were no doubt ensconced in some highly romantic activity at that very moment. The kind of thing she'd dreamed that she and Preston might do one day, after the kids were grown. But she didn't have any intention of dwelling on that thought, since she was more and more grateful to put those ideas behind her and move forward.

Preston had never appreciated her the way she deserved, and Annie would soon find out what that was like. A leopard didn't change his spots, and Preston's spots were well and truly permanent. She could see that now so clearly—how she'd missed it for all those years was astounding.

Hindsight was clarifying, she supposed.

No, she didn't long for those days to return. She was ready for the next phase of her life. She'd found the emails from Preston's solicitor in her junk mail folder, immediately printed them and signed them in front of a witness, then returned them to the solicitor in the mail the next day. She'd believed herself to be divorced for months, but now she finally was. She felt free. Free to move on, to be herself, to love who she wanted.

Before now, she'd felt guilty at the idea of dating Aidan or falling in love again. But now, she was ready. With Preston and Annie on a tropical getaway together, it was the permission she needed to take the next step in her life. If only Aidan was on the same page at the same time. When he'd been ready to dive in, she was reluctant to move too quickly. Now she was in a healthy place with an open heart, but he was busy taking care of his daughter and his business.

She hadn't seen him at all since the dinner with Grace and her mother. He'd missed her call and messaged back that he was hectic with work and hoped to come up for air soon. He'd stopped by the café when Preston visited, but then left again without speaking to her and hadn't taken her calls since. It was all so frustrating and confusing and she didn't know what to do. She ran both hands over her hair and leaned her elbows on the table.

"Hello, darling," Evie said, hurrying over to the table, her red hair swept up into a side ponytail. She bent to kiss Bea on the cheek. "Fancy both of us getting away from the business at the same time. It's practically a miracle."

Bea laughed. "I know, but I'm grateful for small miracles. I needed this."

"Me too."

Taya joined them then, swooping in with her stylishly smooth hair and perfect charcoal pantsuit. "You're both so delicious. I don't know how you do it."

She kissed their cheeks and took a seat with a sigh. "Customers are happy, and I'm exhausted. Let's drink."

When Penny arrived, they were already ordering their second bottle of chardonnay. They were the only customers in the restaurant at the inn, and Penny arched her eyebrows at the sight of them as she walked across the floor to join them. "You're all being very loud."

Evie's guffaw startled Bea. "You're not usually a party pooper."

"What's going on?" Penny sat and tucked her purse beneath the table.

"We're all celebrating," Taya said, leaning back elegantly to cross her legs.

"What are we celebrating?" Penny reached for a glass and filled it with wine.

"Preston is dating one of my best friends from Sydney and came to Coral Island for a romantic getaway and to surprise me with the news that we weren't actually divorced."

Penny gaped. "Wow. Okay."

"And I'm celebrating the imminent demise of my inn," Taya added in a smooth voice.

They all stopped talking at once and turned to stare at her.

Bea frowned. "No, that can't be true."

"Look around," Taya said with a sweeping gesture. "There's no one here but us."

"It's Wednesday. That's all."

"My Dad has built the most amazing, modern, stylish resort at the end of the cove. And I can't blame people for loving it, really—it is fantastic. So they'd rather stay there than here. And he has some crazy chef he flew in from Melbourne, so the food is divine. I visited last night to see what the fuss was all about, and it's the best meal I've had in years." She sighed and picked up her wine glass. "So, drink up, ladies. Because it could be the end for the Blue Shoal Inn very soon."

The group was quiet for a few moments before Penny broke through their reverie.

"I'm so poor that they switched off my electricity and I had to borrow money from Rowan to pay for it to be turned back on."

Bea exclaimed in surprise. "Oh, Penny! You can't just stay quiet about something like that. I would've given you the money."

"I know." Penny patted her arm. "That's why I didn't ask. It's my own fault, and I'm so embarrassed about it. I'm not very good at administration and paperwork. I haven't been keeping track of my expenses and income. I didn't apply for a grant when I should've, and by the time I did, it was already so late that my bank account was basically bare. The grant will come in soon, I hope, and then everything will be okay again. At least for a little while. But I need to get more organised. I say this every year, and then every year, I don't do it." She groaned. "If only I had an assistant or something."

"Don't you have two assistants?" Taya asked.

Penny grunted. "Well, yes, I do. But they only help with the animals, not the paperwork."

"What you really need is an accountant," Bea added. "They keep track of the financials for you. And that way, you can focus on the things you're good at."

"You might have a point," Penny said. "Thanks, Bea. I'll look into that. In the meantime, let's all celebrate that no matter what we're going through, we still have each other."

"Cheers to that," Bea said as they all clinked glasses.

* * *

After the fourth bottle of wine, the world had begun to blur, and Bea was regretting that last glass. That was when Penny suggested they find out more about Rowan's stepfather. What led up to it, Bea had no idea. A conversation about the murder, something to do with the still-open case with no prospect of anyone being charged after all these years.

"He's the only one on the island who might know something," Penny said resolutely.

"That's not true. June Clements is still around too. She's a grouch, but she might be able to tell us more."

"That's true," Penny conceded. "Okay, June and her ex-husband are the only two on the island who can shed light..."

"And Betsy," Bea piped up. "Remember — she was listed as a witness in the newspaper article we read at the library?"

Penny nodded slowly. "Right, and Betsy. So, there are three people."

"Plus my dad," Bea added.

Penny rolled her eyes. "I take it back. There are plenty of people left on the island who might know something. We should talk to every single one of them. See if we can crack the case. My grandmother deserves to have her memory honoured. The very least we can do is figure out who killed her and make sure they pay for their crime."

"It could've been anyone. We don't know who was on the island back then."

"Yes, we do," Taya replied.

All heads swivelled to focus on Taya.

"What do you mean?" Bea asked.

"I did some more reading about the case on my own.

When she died, there was a cyclone along the Queensland northeastern coast. It was in November, and it was the first cyclone of the season. The ferry was damaged in the bad weather, and the island was cut off from the mainland for a month. There was no coming or going. Everyone who was here stayed here for a full month. The police had a complete list of names — I'd say they probably kept it in the case file. If we can get our hands on that, we'd know who was here during the murder."

"Wow, that *is* interesting. But I have no idea how we'd get access to the case file," Evie replied.

Bea shrugged.

"I think we should call Rowan," Evie suggested. "He might know more than he realises."

"I doubt it," Penny replied. "He would've said so. Besides, he wasn't born yet when it happened. None of us were."

"Let's call him anyway," Evie said with a wink.

Bea suppressed a laugh at her friend's obvious attempt at matchmaking. "Penny's his friend. She should call."

Penny shook her head. "I don't know. That's a bit tacky — calling a boy I like after several glasses of wine. I'm not sixteen anymore."

"We didn't drink wine when we were sixteen. Our tastes were much more lowbrow," Taya replied with a laugh.

"You know what I mean."

"Come on, Penny. We want to get to the bottom of this, and I know you do as well. She was your grandmother, after all."

"Fine," Penny conceded. She pulled her mobile phone from her jeans pocket and dialled, then set it on speaker on the table in front of her.

"Hello?" Rowan answered right away.

"Hi, Rowan. It's Penny." Penny's cheeks were already coloured with two pink circles.

"Hi, Pen. How are you?"

"Good. Hey, I'm with the girls."

"Hi, Rowan," they all chimed in unison.

He laughed. "Hi."

"We've been looking into my grandmother's murder, and we wanted to ask you a few questions."

He hesitated. "Me? I'm not sure how much help I can be. I don't know anything about it other than what you've already discovered."

Bea spoke up. "We thought it might be a good idea to talk to each of the people still on the island who were around at the time. Get their memories down on paper."

"Okay," he replied.

"But we don't know where your stepdad lives," Evie added.

"I'm happy to tell you where Buck lives, or lived the last time I heard about him. I don't know what kind of reception you'll get. He was always kind of mean." He gave them his stepfather's address after looking it up on his phone.

"Did your parents ever tell you anything about the murder? Did they mention it in passing or discuss it in front of you?" Penny asked.

He sighed. "Hmmm... Not that I recall. I do remember Mum saying it was a shame, since it really shook your mother's world. They'd been friends, but after the murder, they drifted apart. That was the impression I got, anyway. That your mother was so devastated, she didn't really stay in touch for long, and Mum was saddened by the lost friendship. I believe there were three of them who were friends — Bea's mother as well."

"That's right," Penny replied. "All three of them were close apparently, although obviously Mum was a lot younger than the other two. I think they met doing some kind of pregnancy exercise class and Mum said they took her under their wing.

You'd never have known it later in life, though. They barely spoke when they saw each other at school events. I always thought that was strange."

"Definitely strange," Bea agreed. She hadn't pondered it much at the time, but looking back, she could feel the strained silence between the three mothers who all had children around the same time. They were different ages, with Penny's mother still only in her teens when they were born. But their children were in the same grade at school together years later, and yet the three women barely spoke.

"I think we should visit Buck out at Amity Point. It's not too far from here, and you have the boat, right, Bea? We can drive it around to the point and walk from there. It should be easy enough to find him since there aren't many houses in that area." Penny looked around the table to gauge their reactions.

Bea nodded. "Fine by me. I'm happy to spend more time on the water." She loved going out in the boat. It was her father's, and he'd let her borrow it. She didn't take it out on her own often, but she didn't want to traverse the terrible roads to the inn. Especially since the council had decided it was time to fix the track, and locals were reporting hour-long waiting times for roadworks along the trail.

"Whoa. Maybe you should call first. Like I said, he's a bit of a tyrant." Rowan's voice crackled on the line.

"Where are you?" Penny asked.

"I'm on my way home from climbing Mount Prospect with Aidan."

Just the sound of his name sent a bolt of electricity through Bea's body, momentarily sobering her up. She wanted to climb Mount Prospect with Aidan. It was a small but picturesque mountain, more of a hill really, located in the centre of the island beside Blue Lake. They'd picnicked at the lake several times when they were dating. So many of her favourite memories were bound up in him.

"Okay, we'll let you know how it goes," Penny said. "Thanks, Rowan!" She hung up the phone in the middle of his objections.

"I think he was still talking," Evie pointed out.

Penny blinked. "Was he? Is anyone else's head spinning?"

"Definitely," Bea replied.

"I'm sober," Taya said. "I think I should drive."

Twenty-Two

THE WIND that buffeted the eastern side of the island blew Bea's hair into her face so she could barely see where they were going. Thankfully, Taya had her hair pinned back and stood with both hands on the steering wheel, her face steely, large sunglasses dark against her pale face.

Bea sat beside Evie, who rested her head on Bea's shoulder as they rode. Before long, the waves were too rough, and Evie's head thwacked multiple times on Bea's collarbone before Evie decided to sit up straight.

Bea massaged her shoulder. "You have a hard head. Has anyone ever told you that?"

Evie smiled. "I've heard it a few times. But I think it was meant metaphorically."

They moored the boat in the small marina at Amity Point and climbed the wooden staircase to the streets, where a smattering of charming houses looked out over the headland. It was easy enough to locate the place where Buck Clements lived. It was nestled within a well-tended garden with flower beds and climbing trellises. The house was old but well maintained, and the updated paintwork glistened beneath the afternoon's golden sunshine.

"Well, this wasn't what I was expecting of a man described as a hermit and a tyrant," Bea said, nudging a small garden gnome sporting a red hat.

"No, I thought we'd find a horrible cave or something with an underground pit beside it and a vicious attack dog guarding it." Evie peered along the winding footpath that was cleverly marked out with pretty matching stones.

"That might be a bit hyperbolic," Penny said. "But I know what you mean."

They walked cautiously up the path. Bea bit down on her lower lip. "Do you think this is a good idea?" She was a little more sober now than she had been when they set out, and the previously good idea was beginning to smell a little more like a rotten one.

"It's fine," Taya assured them, striding ahead. "Come on, slowpokes. Try to keep up." Her long legs closed the distance to the house, and Bea jogged along behind her, anxiety turning flips in her gut.

At the front door, Taya raised her fist to knock on the wooden frame. Only a fly screen stood between them and the man who'd terrorised Rowan in his early years. Bea hated to think what that might've entailed. As much pain as she'd gone through in losing her mother, she'd been raised by two parents who not only loved her, but were warm, gentle and kind. The idea of an angry, violent father or stepfather sent a shiver down her spine and made her wish she could go back in time and rescue the young Rowan who'd spoken with a stammer and had always looked so thin and forlorn in their younger years. The memory tugged at her heart strings. Although, she had to admit he hadn't told them any specifics, so perhaps her imagination was exaggerating what'd gone on in their household.

"Hello. Can I help you?" A man walked around the

outside of the house with a shovel in his hands. He wore gardening gloves and a floppy straw hat. His lips were pulled into a wide smile, and his blue eyes twinkled.

Bea was rendered speechless.

"Ah, yes. We're looking for Buck Clements. Does he live here?" Taya said.

The man stepped forward, tugging his hands free of the gloves and shoving them into the front pocket of his denim overalls. "That's me. What can I do you for?" He had a faint American accent and his stomach protruded slightly, but otherwise he was in good shape for his age, which Bea guessed to be around seventy.

"We're friends of Rowan's," Penny said. "We had a few things we wanted to ask you, and he said you wouldn't mind."

Not entirely true, Bea thought, but she wouldn't quibble over the details.

"Oh, Rowan's friends. Why didn't you say so? I'll put the kettle on. Come inside and take a load off." He sounded more Australian with every passing moment.

They followed him inside, where he ushered them into seats. Then he disappeared into the kitchen and soon returned with a platter of cheese, olives and crackers. He sat down opposite Penny with a warm smile.

"You have some questions to ask me? While we wait for the tea, why don't you tell me what you're curious about? Shoot."

Penny outlined the situation and then asked him the question on all of their minds. "Do you know anything at all about my grandmother's murder?"

His eyes narrowed. "Mary Brown. Wow—that name brings it all rushing back. Of course I recall her death. It was a hard time for everyone on the island. Sent a shockwave through the community—something like that doesn't happen often. In fact, I think that's the only time I can recall a murder here."

"Anything you know would be helpful," Bea added. She was still adjusting to the fact that the man in front of her was polite, well-spoken, charming and seemed happy to see them even though he didn't know them. He was a completely different man to the one Rowan had described. Maybe she'd filled in the blanks of his description with her own interpretation. Or perhaps Rowan's teenaged angst had given him a warped perspective. Whatever it was, this man was not the tyrant or the violent, angry villain Rowan had made him out to be.

There was a loud rapping on the doorframe that startled the group.

"Well now, who could that be?" Buck stood to his feet, excused himself and hurried to the front door. He soon returned with Rowan on his trail. "Look who I found."

"Rowan, what are you doing here?" Penny asked.

He arched an eyebrow. "You didn't give me a chance to finish our discussion on the phone."

She stood and embraced him, and he whispered something in her ear that Bea couldn't hear. Then he sat behind Penny, his hand on her shoulder. Bea watched them a moment, wistful. Penny's smile widened, and her face reddened. She was clearly delighted to see him. Bea loved that her friend was so happy. She only wished she could feel the same way instead of the knot of sadness that filled her gut every time she was reminded that she and Aidan had a gulf of missed opportunities between them.

"Let's see. I was just about to answer your question," Buck continued, settling himself back into his armchair. "I recall it was bad weather. A lot of rain, wind, maybe even some hail, if I remember correctly. And Mary, Ruby and the family were all isolated at the beach house over there on the southeastern coast of the island. They have neighbourhoods over there now, but back then, it was just the beach house. Completely alone in the middle of nowhere. We used to go out there to spend time together, swim, surf, fish and snorkel. It's a lovely place, really, although a little too crowded for my tastes now."

"Did they question anyone over the murder?" Bea asked.

"Oh, of course. Everyone. They questioned me and every single other person they could find. It was a big deal. And the population of the island was much smaller back then. So we all had to speak to the authorities, you know, when they managed to make their way here. I believe there was an issue with the ferry, so they had to come by boat through that rain."

"The police came from the mainland?" Taya asked. "So they didn't know any of the people they were interviewing?"

"That's right," Buck replied thoughtfully. "And they had their theories, I guess. But it never amounted to anything. I knew most of the people who lived here back then, and I couldn't imagine a single one of them doing it. Although obviously someone was responsible. It's hard to believe, that's for certain."

"Where in America are you from?" Evie asked.

He smiled. "Indiana, born and bred."

"When did you move to Coral Island?"

He scratched his balding pate. "Let's see. It must've been around nineteen eighty-two. Something like that, anyhow."

"Do you miss it?" Penny asked.

"Not really. I did for a while, but it's been so long now, I don't think about it much. And who could find a better place to live than Coral Island?"

They all smiled at that. Bea agreed—she couldn't imagine living anywhere else now that she was home. It was the only place she truly felt like herself now that her life in Sydney was over.

After they'd exhausted all of their questions, they rose to

leave. The women waited outside while Rowan and his stepfather spoke together in low voices in the entry to the small house. Finally, the two men embraced, and Rowan stepped outside to join them with red-rimmed eyes. He took Penny by the hand silently, and the two of them walked up the pathway towards the road where his SUV was parked.

"Well, thank you. Goodbye!" Bea called to Buck, hurrying after them.

"He was different to what I thought he'd be," Evie said, coming up alongside her.

"Very," Bea agreed.

"What do you think that was about?" Taya asked, dipping her head in Rowan's direction.

"Hopefully, mending fences," Bea replied. "Sometimes teens misjudge people. Happens all the time."

"It seems his stepfather wasn't the monster he thought. In fact, he's extremely friendly, from what we saw today," Evie said. "It's nice to see something work out for a change."

"Yes, it is," Taya agreed.

Twenty-Three

THE NEXT DAY dawned with a growl and a hiss. Rain spat against the cottage windows, and the sun barely rose, hidden behind a swathe of dark clouds. Bea slept late and called in to the café to let them know she wouldn't be in. She had a sore throat and a headache, and they weren't expecting many customers. She knew the casual staff could manage without her, and all she wanted to do was to stay in bed and hide under the covers.

She missed her kids. She missed Aidan. She wasn't sure how she was going to get through this slump. He wasn't returning her calls. She'd seen him driving his truck in the distance one time since he'd rushed away from the café the day Preston visited. All she wanted to do was to see him face-to-face and tell him she was finally divorced and ready to move on, but he wouldn't give her the chance. And she had to believe, finally, that it was because he didn't want to take their relationship to the next level. She should let go of the dream that she'd harboured in her heart of them reconciling after all these years and sailing into the blissful sunset of life together hand in hand.

Feeling eminently sorry for herself, she trudged up the hill in her rain gear and knocked on her father's door. He opened it and she stepped inside, then hung up her dripping raincoat and shucked off her boots.

"Hi, Dad," she said.

"Wow, things must be bad," he quipped, his eyes sparkling.

"How can you tell?"

"You sound like they just reported a devastating meteor is headed to earth," he replied.

She grunted her approval at that, but couldn't muster up a laugh. Then she headed to the kitchen. "Do you have tea?"

He followed her. "Every kind you might want."

"That blue flowery stuff will do. With some honey. My throat is killing me."

"Are you saying you brought the plague into my home?" he asked with one eyebrow raised, opening the cupboard to pull out a tin of tea and setting it on the bench. "Why would you do that?"

"Sorry, Dad. I'm sure you'll be fine. I need honey, though. Have you got any of that organic stuff?"

He chuckled. "Go sit in the living room by the fire. I'll bring your tea."

Bea shuffled to the living room, picked up a blanket from the couch and slung it around her shoulders before sitting, hunchbacked, by the fire roaring in the hearth. She wasn't sure why her father had lit a fire on a tropical island, but she wasn't about to question his wisdom. It was exactly what she needed. Her heartbreak was reflected in the storm raging outside.

Finally, Dad brought a pot of tea and set it on the table beside her. He poured two cups, swirled in some honey, then sat across from her.

"You doing okay, sweetie?"

She grunted and scowled. "Depends what you consider okay."

"Fine, I'll start with something easier. How's the throat?"

"The honey and tea are helping."

"Good," he replied, taking a sip of his own.

"Have you heard anything else from the doctor?" she asked as she held a hand up to her throat. Did she have a fever? It certainly felt like it — her entire body ached from top to toe.

"Oh, didn't I tell you? I went to the mainland to see him yesterday."

She sat up straight. "No, I didn't realise. I would've taken you, Dad. You should've told me."

"It was fine—Aidan took me. We arranged it last week."

Her mouth fell open. Aidan took him? Why? How? So many questions, but she could only gape.

Dad sipped his tea again. "Yeah, we were talking last week when he came over to help me fix my lawnmower."

"He did what?"

"It wasn't working, and I know he's good with engines. My eyesight isn't what it used to be. So I gave him a call, and he came right over. We chatted for a while about my health, and when I mentioned the appointment, he said he had to go to town anyway and why didn't he give me a lift as well? So, I agreed. He said he would stop by the café and let you know. Didn't he?"

Bea slapped a palm to her forehead and squeezed her eyes shut. That was why he came to see her. And then when Preston was there, embracing her, he must've been confused. He should've spoken to her instead of running away. She could've explained everything.

"He did stop by," she said. "But we didn't have a chance to speak."

"Oh," Dad replied. "Never mind. He took me to see the doctor. We had lunch, too, at this lovely Italian place. He insisted on paying. The doctor gave me a prescription, and Aidan took me to fill it, so I'm all set. I started on the medication yesterday, and the doc assures me it'll fix me right up so I don't have to worry about more strokes any time soon."

"I'm glad he was able to figure it all out and get you onto medication right away," Bea said. "That's a big relief."

Bea pondered his words as she drank her tea. She and Aidan had to find the time to have a conversation. His kindness brought tears to her eyes. Her father was one of the most important people in her life. Aidan knew how worried about him she'd been and he'd stepped in to help without asking for anything in return. Without seeking her approval or recognition.

"Why did he do it, do you think?"

Dad hesitated. "He's a good man. And a good friend."

"Yes, he is. Isn't he?"

Twenty-Four

PENNY HAD RECEIVED a call from a woman reporting an injured animal she'd seen while out bushwalking. The road to the place described by the woman who'd called her was bumpy and riddled with potholes.

Penny slowed the pace of her SUV and traversed an enormous crater, then pulled the vehicle to the side of the road. This was the place, according to the caller. She'd spotted an injured bush possum or ringtail possum—it was impossible to tell, since the woman couldn't identify either type. The animal was injured and needed help.

"But don't worry," she'd ended the call by saying. "The possum won't go anywhere since it's tangled in wire which is ensnared around a fallen log."

Penny shook her head as she climbed out of the car and retrieved the animal transportation cage from the back seat. The least the caller could've done was to stay with the creature to guide her to its location. But no, she had to get back home for lunch. Never mind—Penny was certain she'd be able to locate the animal. It might take the rest of the day, but she'd manage it. She couldn't bear the idea of leaving it out there alone overnight, tangled around a tree trunk.

As she walked along the single-lane dirt track, she suddenly realised just how far out of the way the woman's directions had taken her. Perhaps she should call for some backup. The other staff from the refuge were busily feeding and ministering to animals, but one of the girls had gone to Penny's house to nurse a baby joey that needed regular monitoring and care between naps. Perhaps Penny could catch her there and ask her to bring the other vehicle to her location just in case Penny couldn't manage on her own. She dialled her home number, and a male voice answered the call.

"Hello. Who is this?" She couldn't imagine who might be inside her house in the middle of the day.

"It's Rowan. How's things?"

Her mind raced as she attempted to come up with a reasonable solution to the question, what was Rowan Clements doing inside her house?

"I'm fine, thanks, Rowan. Um... What are you doing there?"

"Why are you calling your own house? That's the real question."

"I was hoping to speak to Alison. Is she there?"

"Nope. She's not. She's back at the refuge."

"Okay." This made no sense whatsoever. Alison wasn't there, but Rowan was?

"I pulled up outside your house and found Alison opening the front door. She said she was here to feed the joey, and I suggested I do it for her since she looked harried. So she went back to the refuge, and I'm here with the little dude, giving him his milk bottle. He's pretty darned cute, I have to say. By the way, where are you?"

Penny's heart skipped a beat. Rowan was feeding the joey

at her house at that very moment. She wished she could be there to take in the vision of the two of them together, but instead she was standing ankle-deep in a mud puddle in the middle of the bush somewhere on the island.

"I'm not sure exactly where I am, but I'm going to send you a pin drop on the map. Can you please call Alison at the refuge and ask her to meet me at that location? I'm picking up an injured animal, and I'm out in the middle of the bush alone. I thought it might be a good idea to have her come too just in case something goes wrong."

"I can come and help," Rowan said. "I've almost finished feeding the little joey here, and then I'll be right over."

"No, that's okay. You don't have to do that. It's what I pay Alison to do."

"I'm happy to."

"No, really. Alison will be fine, but thanks for the offer. It's very kind of you. And you didn't have to feed the joey for me. I'm sorry you got roped into it." She loved that he was willing to help, but he was on vacation. He didn't need to be working for her. She was certain he had better things to do with his time.

She sent him the pin drop, then held the phone to her ear again. "Did you get that?"

Just then, the phone beeped, and the line went dead. She looked at the screen — the battery was low, and the bars along the top were gone. There was absolutely no signal.

"Blasted thing," she said, shaking the phone. Not that it would help. She shoved it deep into her pocket, picked up the animal cage again and trudged forwards into the bush. She'd simply have to handle it alone.

An hour later, Penny finally located the ring-tailed possum and managed to get it free of the wire tangled around it and into the cage using a pair of thick gloves. She closed the cage and breathed a sigh of relief.

"There you go. Now to find my car and get out of here." The problem was that she'd walked back and forth so many times looking for the animal, she wasn't entirely sure which direction to march.

She'd have to do her best to follow her own tracks. It might be a long, winding way back, but at least she'd make it eventually.

After a while, she came across a creek that she most definitely did not recall crossing on her way in. She slumped down beside the creek with a sigh. There was still no signal on her phone, and soon the sun would begin to set. She might end up spending the night out there alone in the bush. Thankfully, she'd brought a water bottle with her, and a torch. But she had nothing to eat and no emergency blanket. At least it was still fairly warm on the island so she wouldn't have to worry about exposure.

She let herself rest to catch her breath for a few minutes, flexed her tired arm, and picked up the cage again. "Sorry, little buddy. I'll get you back to the refuge as soon as I can manage to dress those wounds and give you something to eat." The poor animal looked as though it'd been stuck by the tree for a long time and had very little energy. At least it wasn't making a fuss about the trip back to the car.

She wasn't going to panic. She'd find the vehicle eventually. It was only a matter of time until she stumbled upon the track she'd driven in on. Surely.

Her only hope was that the pin drop she'd sent to Rowan had made it through to his phone. And that when she didn't show up for work the next day, someone would report her missing. That is, if she didn't make it back to the car before nightfall.

She stood to her feet and climbed back up the creek bank. Halfway up the rise, she stumbled over a fallen tree branch, tripped and fell. She dropped the cage and tried to struggle back to her feet, but her body was moving faster than her legs could manage and she tumbled over a large log. Her leg made a horrible snapping sound, and then pain rocked her calf and up into her body. She came to a standstill in the dirt and leaves, agony radiating all over her body. Then leaned to one side and heaved violently.

With a groan of pain, she sat up and felt along her leg. There was nothing obviously wrong with it, but the anguish triggered tears to fall in rivulets down both cheeks. She sniffled into her shirt sleeve, braced herself and attempted to stand. But it was no use. She couldn't do it.

"Argh!" she screamed as her leg crumpled beneath her.

It was broken. She was sure of it. The possum cage was further up the hill out of reach, rolled over onto one side. She hoped the animal hadn't been further injured by her clumsiness. With a grunt of pain, she lay on her back on the sloping bank of the creek and looked up through the tree branches to the sky overhead. It'd turned a lovely shade of pink mixed with gold. It would be dark soon, and she was going nowhere.

It was less than an hour before she heard the first shout. She sat bolt upright, then grimaced as pain rushed up her leg. There it was again. It was definitely a man's voice, shouting nearby in the bush.

It was entirely dark now. Crickets sang along the water's edge. The creek bubbled loudly. For a moment she wondered if it'd been her imagination, but she was certain she'd heard a voice. She supposed she could be hallucinating. There was only one way to find out for certain which it was.

"Hello?" she yelled. Her voice was thin and raspy. She

cleared her throat and tried again. "Cooee!" This time, her voice ran out loud and clear.

"Cooee!" came the quick reply. Tears filled her eyes. She responded in kind again. The call went back and forth between them until Rowan appeared at the top of the creek bank. He hurried down to where she lay and squatted beside her.

"I've been looking everywhere for you. What's wrong?"

"I broke my leg," she sobbed. She was so glad to see him, she could kiss him right there on the spot.

"Okay, well, let's get you out of here. Hold on."

She laced her arms around his neck and he lifted her gently, careful not to move her leg too much.

"Don't forget the possum," she said.

He rolled his eyes. "Really? How am I supposed to manage that?"

"Fine. Let me carry it," she said.

"Can't you set it free?"

She considered. "It might be better for the animal, actually. You're right. I should've done that earlier. I was trying to be a hero. Open the gate and let it out."

He set her down on the ground again and opened the cage, and the possum soon emerged. It seemed to have perked up since she freed it earlier and quickly scurried away into the night. He closed the cage.

"Let's go, Pen. You can worry about the cage some other time."

He lifted her in his arms again, and she leaned against his chest. Her hands were linked behind his neck, and the steady beat of his heart pounded a rhythm in her ear. She felt as though she could stay in that place forever.

It didn't take him long to locate the cars. He loaded her into his and hurried around to start the engine.

"Are you warm enough?"

"Fine, thank you," she said. She'd gotten a little stiff lying on the cold, wet creek bank. But now that she was in the vehicle, all that was behind her. She was simply happy to be seated in a comfortable chair.

He switched on the car's heater. "Just in case."

She smiled. Who would've known he was so caring and thoughtful? Certainly not her. She'd never have guessed that Rowan Clements, her childhood nemesis, would've been the one to rescue her, to carry her through the bush, to make sure she was comfortable. The about-face her life had taken in recent weeks had left her with emotional whiplash. But even while in physical pain, she was blissfully happy, which was an emotion she hadn't felt in a very long time.

Rowan drove her to the small hospital in Kellyville and helped her into a wheelchair to take her inside. They whisked her away for x-rays and tests and informed her they would keep her at the hospital for several days since they had to perform surgery on her leg. She wanted to be frustrated by the interruption to her schedule, but she couldn't manage anything other than a request to please go to bed. She was exhausted.

It was midnight by the time she finally found her way to a room, a nurse pushing her wheelchair. The nurse flicked on a light and found Rowan fast asleep in a small blue armchair in the corner of the room. The woman smiled as she helped Penny into the bed.

"Looks like someone was worried about you."

She turned off the light when she left, and Penny watched Rowan snoring lightly where he lay, crumpled at odd angles in the chair. She studied the line of his chiselled jaw and the length of his athletic legs. The way his hair fell across his forehead and the smile lines around the outside of his mouth. He was handsome, but there was more to her attraction than simply his looks. He was good and kind, thoughtful and caring.

She couldn't imagine living without him now, even though he'd only upended her life a few short weeks earlier. She nestled down into her covers, careful not to knock her newly bound leg against anything, and fell to sleep with the outline of his face etched across her mind's eye.

Twenty-Five

THE DRIVE TO Aidan's house in the dark seemed far too long to Beatrice. She was in a hurry. There was no way for her to know how Aidan would react to her rushing to see him, but she'd been in bed sick for two days and today she finally felt up to driving. Her head no longer spun every time she stood, the fever was gone and her throat didn't burn like it was on fire. She had to see him.

Ever since Dad told her about what Aidan had done for him, she hadn't been able to stop thinking about it. Even if all she managed to do was thank him, then she'd do that. But she hoped he would hear her out — there was no reason for them to be apart any longer.

Grace had moved home with her mother. Bea had given Aidan time to manage his thoughts and emotions, to work out his relationship with Grace. She'd given him the space he wanted, hadn't pushed him to reconsider. At least, until tonight. But she had to know — did he want space to process his feelings, or did he push her away for another reason?

She pulled into his driveway, her heart pounding. As she

climbed out, she saw that his bedroom light was still on, but the rest of the house lay in darkness. When she knocked on the door, his golden retriever barked dully from some room in the house, probably Aidan's bedroom. Before long, she heard his footsteps on the stairs, and he tugged open the door, his tousled hair freshly wet from the shower.

"Bumble Bea?" He looked confused. "Were we planning to meet? I must've forgotten..."

"No, we didn't have plans," she said. "I'm sorry it's so late."

"It's fine. Come on in."

She followed him into the house, her pulse racing. It was now or never. She had to confront him and learn the truth or she'd never be satisfied.

"Would you like a coffee? Tea? Wine?" He opened the refrigerator, stared inside, then combed his hair with one hand. He seemed agitated. He wore nothing but a pair of board shorts. His muscled chest flexed as he turned to look at her, the question still on his face.

She nodded. "Wine would be lovely. Thanks."

He poured them each a glass of chardonnay from an already open bottle. "Should we go outside?"

"Okay."

They carried their wine out onto the deck. She could hear the ocean shushing the creatures of the night with its rhythmic voice, but couldn't see it through the gloaming.

They sat near one another and sipped in silence. Finally, Bea spoke.

"Dad told me you took him to the doctor."

He leaned forward, elbows on his thighs. "Oh, yeah. Sounds like everything's going to be just fine."

"Thank you," she said. "You didn't have to do that."

"I care about him too," he said softly.

"I know, and that's one of the many reasons why I love you."

He straightened. "You what?"

She swallowed. There was no backing down now. "I love you."

"You do?"

"Yes, and I need to know how you feel about me. Because there's no reason we can't be together anymore. And the longer this separation takes, the worse I feel." She stood and paced to the deck railing, leaning on it to stare into the darkness.

He followed her, turned her to face him, then rested his hands on her lower back, arms encircling her. "I like hearing that."

"I'm glad," she said, her stomach a knot of nerves.

"And I agree — there's no reason for us to be apart any longer. When Grace went back to live with her mother, I convinced myself you'd moved on. That I'd lost my chance, it was too late. Then I saw you embracing that man at the café..." His eyes clouded and nostrils flared.

"That was Preston. He was hugging me goodbye," she said.

His eyes narrowed. "Your ex-husband?"

"Yes, with his new girlfriend."

"Oh." He smiled. "I wish I'd stuck around to ask."

"So do I," she said with a shake of her head. "That's a rule from now on. If this thing is going to work, no more assumptions. We have to talk about everything. And trust one another."

He leaned closer. "I can live with those terms."

"So, are you ready to give this another try?" She asked the question shyly as though she was that teenaged girl all over again, asking Aidan Whitlock to give her his heart.

"With everything I've got," he whispered as he kissed the

tip of her nose. "Oh, and I love you too, Bumble Bea. Always have. Always will."

His hands cupped her face, cradling it gently as he stared into her eyes. The depth of the emotion in his gaze made her heart stand still. Then his lips found hers, and the world stood still too.

Twenty-Six

THE CAST on her leg made getting around difficult, but Penny was grateful it wasn't a full leg cast. And at least it was removable — a feature that became increasingly convenient when she was itchy. She hobbled through the living room to the front door and pulled it open just as Rob pushed his key towards the knob.

He laughed. "Well, thanks."

She stepped back. "What are you doing here?"

"Nice to see you too, Pen. I finished my job early." He walked into the house and shut the door behind him.

"Sorry. It is nice to see you," she said, giving him a hug.

He looked her up and down. "What on earth happened to you?"

She sighed. "Come on. We'll have a cup of tea, and I'll tell you all about it."

They discussed her accident and Rowan coming to her rescue. She watched his face as she spoke in an attempt to figure out how he felt about the whole thing. It was no secret that he was adamantly against any one of his friends dating his sister. But that'd been a long time ago. The fact that they'd

195

fought over it before he left the island the last time was still on her mind, though.

When she finished speaking, he leaned forward in his chair. "Are the two of you an item now?"

She tensed. "What if we were?"

He shook his head. "I suppose if it's serious…"

"It's not," she said. "Well, not yet. We're not even official. I just… Well, I like him."

He sat back, studying her through deep brown eyes. "Okay."

"Okay what?" she asked, her stomach flip-flopping over the anticipation of what he might say.

"Okay — you like each other. So, I think you should see where it might go. I had my reasons for not wanting you to see him, but it's too late for that. You're already beyond that point."

"Anything I should know about?" If there was a genuine issue, she'd prefer to know now.

He hesitated, his eyes troubled. Then shook his head. "No, it's probably nothing. He's a great guy. I hope you'll be happy together."

"Really?" she squealed.

He nodded again, smiling. She threw her arms around his neck, knocking him off his chair. He caught himself before he fell, then extricated himself from her arms. "I see how you managed to break your leg now."

She sighed, a wide grin splitting her face in two. "You've made my day."

"I'm glad," he said. "Any chance you've got a slice of cake hidden around here somewhere? I'm starved."

The cake was soon served, and she listened while he updated her on his work situation, his son and everything that'd happened since they last saw one another. He hadn't really kept her up-to-date since they'd parted on bad terms.

And she realised how much she'd missed him and was desperate for some brother-sister bonding time.

"So, I've decided to move back to Coral Island," he said all of a sudden.

Penny hadn't expected it, and the words stole her breath away.

He watched her gaping for a moment, then laughed. "Well, say something."

"I don't know what to say. I didn't think you'd ever do that. What about Julian?"

"I'm doing it for him. I can't get partial custody while I'm moving all over the place for work. This way, I'll live in one place and he can come and stay with me during the holidays. I've already worked it out with Jacqui. She said she's fine with it. In fact, I think she was glad."

Penny smiled. "I'm really happy for you, Rob. Where will you stay?"

His smile faded. "Well ... here, of course."

Beatrice felt as though she now spent her life moving around in a state of bliss. He loved her. She hadn't expected it to go so well when she'd driven over to his house a week earlier, but ever since then, they'd seen each other every day. They'd been to the movies, they'd had a snorkelling date, they'd surfed several mornings together and they'd even eaten takeaway on his back deck looking out over the ocean under a canopy of stars.

It was perfect, romantic and everything she'd hoped for.

The only thing bothering her was the mystery surrounding the murder. Each of the women had agreed to talk to one person they knew had been around when Mary was killed. They had to get to the bottom of it. She could sense the urgency in Penny, Taya and Evie as well. It was always just beneath the surface for each of them, this tangible curiosity and excitement over what they might find. And it'd all begun with the old photographs she'd found hidden in her cottage wall when she and Danita were renovating it.

She pulled her car to a stop outside Betsy's florist shop and climbed out, carrying a tray of freshly baked scones. If she must interrogate her friend over a murder that happened forty-five years earlier, the least she could do was to bribe her with baked goods.

Inside the store, she found Betsy reading a magazine, half-moon glasses perched on the end of her nose. Beside her, Sam sat on a small chair, leaning a colouring book on the counter. She wore a brand-new dress in pink, with her hair neatly combed into a ponytail. She smiled at Bea and showed her the picture she was colouring, which Bea exclaimed over in suitable tones of amazement. Betsy put down her magazine.

"Well, look who the cat dragged in." She greeted Bea with a kiss on the cheek. "Nice to see you. How's things?"

Bea blushed. "Aidan and I are seeing each other. Again."

Betsy's eyes widened. "Well, that is good news. I'm happy for you both."

"Thank you. I'm happy too. So happy, I baked." She handed Betsy the tray of scones.

"Well now, ain't that sweet of you? I love some home-baked scones with jam and cream. One of my favourite local treats."

"I'm glad," Bea said. "Actually, I'm buttering you up because I wanted to ask you a few questions about something that happened a long time ago."

Bea pulled the envelope of photographs out of her handbag and set them on the bench in front of Betsy. Betsy tugged them free and stared at them, her face growing pale.

"I'm looking into Mary Brown's murder. Trying to find

out who killed her, to maybe get some justice for Penny and her family."

"That sounds like quite the undertaking."

"Right. Well, I noticed that you were listed as a witness in the newspaper report. And I hoped you might be able to tell me what you saw. And what you remember about the case."

Betsy met her gaze briefly, then looked back down at the photos, pushing each aside one by one with a fingertip.

"Do you know these people?" Bea asked.

"Sure," Betsy replied. "I know them. Those are Penny's folks."

"That's right. And Rowan Clements' family as well."

"Yeah, June and Buck. I know them. They're lovely photos. Where did you get them? I don't think I've ever seen them before."

"I found them hidden in the wall of my cottage. The kitchen wall. When Dani and I were renovating, we pulled out this roll of film, and I decided to get it processed. It's what put us onto the whole murder mystery."

Betsy's eyes widened. "That's what was hidden."

"What do you mean?" Bea asked.

"By your mother."

Bea's stomach lurched. "My mother hid the film?"

"I'm guessing so. I saw her go into the cottage with a bag and come out empty-handed. It's when she dropped the music box. I was taking a walk—I had a dog back then, you know—and I was walking her by your property and down to the beach. They were building that cottage of yours by the water, and I thought I'd take a look.

"That's when I saw her. She stumbled out of there like she'd seen a ghost. When she ran away, she dropped the music box. I put it in my pocket and meant to get it back to her, but I forgot all about it for a long while and didn't wear that cardigan again for an age. It was a particularly cold day that day, which we don't get much of here on the island. When I finally pulled it out to wear years later and stuck my hand in the pocket, well, it was too late. Your mother was gone."

Bea clapped a hand to her mouth. "I can't believe it. All this time, I've wondered who could've put the photos there and why. Now I know the answer to the first question — or at least, it seems likely."

"She'd had her head down and was in a kind of hurry. And when she came out of the cottage, she didn't have the bag with her. I figured she'd left it there for some reason."

"Why would she do that?" Bea asked, her brow furrowed. "Why would she go into her own cottage and hide a roll of film?"

"Oh, the cottage wasn't hers at the time," Betsy replied. "Your father bought it—he didn't build it. Don't you remember?"

Bea nodded slowly. "That's right — I did know that. I forgot for a moment. So, if they didn't build it, who did?"

Betsy smiled and stabbed a finger at the photograph in front of her. "Buck Clements did."

Continue the series...

Ready to read book 3 in the *Coral Island* series so you can keep following Beatrice, Aidan and the rest of the Coral Island crew? Buy the next book in this series!

· · ·

Looking for a fun **new series to read?**

Check out "Cottage on Oceanview Lane", book 1 in the *Emerald Cove* series: When Cindy discovers a heartbreaking betrayal, her daughter Sarah steps in to help pick up the pieces — leaving behind her book editing job in the city to run the family beachside café. Can the ocean breeze bring them both a fresh start?

Want to find out **about all of my new releases?** You can get on my VIP reader list by subscribing via my website, and you'll also get a ***free book***.

Also by Lilly Mirren

WOMEN'S FICTION

CORAL ISLAND SERIES

The Island

After twenty five years of marriage and decades caring for her two children, on the evening of their vow renewal, her husband shocks her with the news that he's leaving her.

The Beach Cottage

Beatrice is speechless. It's something she never expected — a secret daughter. She and Aidan have only just renewed their romance, after decades apart, and he never mentioned a child. Did he know she existed?

The Blue Shoal Inn

Taya's inn is in trouble. Her father has built a fancy new resort in Blue Shoal and hired a handsome stranger to manage it. When the stranger offers to buy her inn and merge it with the resort, she wants to hate him but when he rescues a stray dog her feelings for him change.

THE WARATAH INN SERIES

The Waratah Inn

Wrested back to Cabarita Beach by her grandmother's sudden death, Kate Summer discovers a mystery buried in the past that changes everything.

One Summer in Italy

Reeda leaves the Waratah Inn and returns to Sydney, her husband, and her thriving interior design business, only to find her marriage in tatters. She's lost sight of what she wants in life and can't recognise the person she's become.

The Summer Sisters

Set against the golden sands and crystal clear waters of Cabarita Beach three sisters inherit an inn and discover a mystery about their grandmother's past that changes everything they thought they knew about their family...

Christmas at The Waratah Inn

Liz Cranwell is divorced and alone at Christmas. When her friends convince her to holiday at The Waratah Inn, she's dreading her first Christmas on her own. Instead she discovers that strangers can be the balm to heal the wounds of a lonely heart in this heartwarming Christmas story.

EMERALD COVE SERIES

Cottage on Oceanview Lane

When a renowned book editor returns to her roots, she

rediscovers her strength & her passion in this heartwarming novel.

Seaside Manor Bed & Breakfast

The Seaside Manor Bed and Breakfast has been an institution in Emerald Cove for as long as anyone can remember. But things are changing and Diana is nervous about what the future might hold for her and her husband, not to mention the historic business.

Bungalow on Pelican Way

Moving to the Cove gave Rebecca De Vries a place to hide from her abusive ex. Now that he's in jail, she can get back to living her life as a police officer in her adopted hometown working alongside her intractable but very attractive boss, Franklin.

Chalet on Cliffside Drive

At forty-four years of age, Ben Silver thought he'd never find love. When he moves to Emerald Cove, he does it to support his birth mother, Diana, after her husband's sudden death. But then he meets Vicky.

Christmas in Emerald Cove

The Flannigan family has been through a lot together. They've grown and changed over the years and now have a blended and extended family that doesn't always see eye to eye. But this Christmas they'll learn that love can overcome all of the pain and differences of the past in this inspiring Christmas tale.

HOME SWEET HOME SERIES

Home Sweet Home

Trina is starting over after a painful separation from her husband of almost twenty years. Grief and loss force her to return to her hometown where she has to deal with all of the things she left behind to rebuild her life, piece by piece; a hometown she hasn't visited since high school graduation.

No Place Like Home

Lisa never thought she'd leave her high-profile finance job in the city to work in a small-town bakery. She also never expected to still be single in her forties.

HISTORICAL FICTION

Beyond the Crushing Waves

An emotional standalone historical saga. Two children plucked from poverty & forcibly deported from the UK to Australia. Inspired by true events. An unforgettable tale of loss, love, redemption & new beginnings.

Under a Sunburnt Sky

Inspired by a true story. Jan Kostanski is a normal Catholic boy in Warsaw when the nazis invade. He's separated from his neighbours, a Jewish family who he considers kin, by the ghetto wall. Jan and his mother decide that they will do whatever it takes to save their Jewish friends from certain death. The unforgettable tale of an everyday family's fight against evil, and the unbreakable bonds of their love.

MYSTERIES

White Picket Lies

Fighting the demons of her past Toni finds herself in the midst of a second marriage breakdown at forty seven years of age. She struggles to keep depression at bay while doing her best to raise a wayward teenaged son and uncover the identity of the killer.

In this small town investigation, it's only a matter of time until friends and neighbours turn on each other.

About the Author

Lilly Mirren is an Amazon top 20, Audible top 15 and USA Today Bestselling author who has sold over one million copies of her books worldwide. She lives in Brisbane, Australia with her husband and three children.

She always dreamed of being a writer and is now living that dream. Her books combine heartwarming storylines with realistic characters readers can't get enough of.

Her debut series, The Waratah Inn, set in the delightful Cabarita Beach, hit the *USA Today* Bestseller list and since then, has touched the hearts of hundreds of thousands of readers across the globe.

Made in the USA
Middletown, DE
25 October 2022

13511553R00119